We
need
to
talk

First published 2015 by Jurassic London
SW8 1XN, Great Britain
www.jurassic-london.com

978-0-9928435-6-4 (Trade)
978-0-9928435-5-7 (eBook)

Cover by Lisa Wright
www.kindredagency.com

Edited by Jared Shurin

Printed and bound by Imprint Academic, Exeter, UK

We need to talk

Stories about difficult conversations

Introduced by Milly Johnson

Selected by Kindred

In aid of The Eve Appeal

Contents

Introduction

One of the most difficult things to write in fiction is the 'tricky conversation'. We've all had them in real life – not knowing whether or not to say something for the best and then rehearsing it beforehand, only for it to come out totally differently to how we planned. They're always awkward, never eloquent and often half-way through them, we wish we had never opened our mouths. But there are occasions when we just need to say things, however uncomfortable, clumsy or embarrassing they are because they're problems which will only get worse if we don't confront them – but they could get better if we do.

Sometimes in life we need to grit our teeth, open our mouths and face a problem head on and nowhere does this make more sense than in health issues. Talking about gynaecological issues should not be embarrassing. We should all know our own bodies and not rationalise away any changes they are flagging up but our brains are too scared to acknowledge. We should be aware of anything we find different about the way our body engine runs and have it checked out. They may be perfectly normal changes and then we can stop worrying, can't we?

Whenever I have to write a tricky conversation, I make sure that however calmly and thoroughly it is planned, that – depending on the character – it could fire out of a mouth with an accompaniment of tears and a flood of emotion, but it doesn't matter. Some things – in life as well as books – are NOT better left unsaid.

Milly Johnson

Cowardy Custard

by

Tim Major

I have this memory from my childhood, of a drizzly May day that turned to a heat that fizzled the water right off the grass. My dad took me to the fair at Headington. I was seven, maybe eight, and a Disney-princess-hating tomboy. We ate the greasiest of beefburgers, then dad gave me a thumbs-up as I churned the food in my stomach on the bungee trampoline, then he laughed and patted my back when I puked it all onto the ground behind the ghost train.

I adored my dad.

The fairground rides were just preamble, though. We'd come for the magic.

Dad had bought me a toy magic set the Christmas before. He spent Saturday after Saturday beside me at the kitchen table, deciphering instructions. He let me tap the wand and therefore be the real author of each illusion.

We took our places on the hay bale seats. The crowds were still in the main arena, watching a dog walk on his hind legs. Dad and I made our guesses about the tricks, based on the props we glimpsed on a red-painted cabinet. The old cup-and-ball trick! The changing-length rope!

When the dog got tired of performing, or when the crowd got tired of the dog, other children arrived. Dad stood with the other parents at the side of the roped-off area. I spread my elbows as wide as possible to stop other kids encroaching on my space. I needed to see the show, sleight of hand and all, and I needed to see dad, too.

We exchanged looks when the magician appeared from the back of the tent. His yellow-and-black striped jacket made him appear more Butlins entertainer than mysterious conjuror. Dad raised his eyebrows and shrugged.

The magician did a pantomime double-take. 'Good grief! What a terrifying bunch!'

Children around me giggled. I scowled.

The magician turned away and whispered into his wireless microphone. 'Be brave, Custard, be brave.' He spun around and flung his arms wide. 'My name is C-C-Cowardy Custard!'

Streamers burst from his sleeves. Everyone applauded, except me.

The streamers weren't streamers after all. They were balloons, yet to be inflated. He grabbed a few from the ground and made a show of blowing them up, inspecting each one as if bamboozled by its shape and potential. With a flourish, he tied together three balloons to make a huge, bulbous baby's dummy.

This show was for kids. I was ready to leave.

Cowardy Custard held up the balloon dummy. Children around me stood on their hay bales to try and grab it. The magician moved over to where the parents stood. He handed the dummy to my dad. I was mortified, but dad played along. He pretended to suck the dummy, then his thumb. Good old dad. What a sport.

The magician got down to business. He juggled coloured balls, then inserted them into a tube. A sleeve went over the tube. When he lifted it, the green, orange and red balls had changed position.

With that, I was sold.

Next up was the changing-length rope trick. Dad had attempted it at home, but it had been nothing like this. I watched the magician's hands carefully, keeping my eyes on his sleeves. When he pretended to trip over and leant on the red-painted cabinet, I didn't fall for the distraction. But the trick worked, all the same. The three different lengths of rope became one long string, then three equal lengths.

I glanced over at dad. He puffed out his cheeks: This guy's pretty good.

Several times, Cowardy Custard asked for volunteers from the audience. I leapt up and down, pushing my neighbours aside. Each time, he picked someone else. Maybe he knew he'd get better reactions from younger children. Maybe I looked like a smartarse who just might just ruin his show.

One of the volunteers held an empty glass bowl and nearly dropped it when a sprinkling of glitter somehow became a live goldfish. Another two children guided Maltesers along an extended tape measure and into the mouth of a waiting third.

'For my next illusion,' Cowardy Custard said, resting one hand on the shoulder of his latest volunteer, 'My young friend here will need an ordinary ring from a member of the audience. I'm going to pick on you again, sir! I imagine you're married?'

He pointed at my dad. Dad gave an over-the-top groan. He took off his wedding ring and handed it over. The crowd applauded. He mimed biting his nails. What a sport.

The volunteer boy held up the cloth bag that contained the ring. When asked, he bashed it up and down on the cabinet top. He watched as the magician hit it with a hammer. On Cowardy Custard's instruction, he removed one layer after another from a Russian doll, then verified that the ring was inside the smallest doll. My dad received the ring with a solemn bow and the crowd whooped.

I sulked. Most of the segments that involved volunteers were more pantomime than magic show. When Cowardy Custard asked for three children for his grand finale, I didn't even raise my hand. Two boys and a girl—each around six years old, I guess—stepped under the lifted rope barrier to join him.

The magician knelt before the volunteers. He lowered his voice to a whisper. 'Before we start, I need to ask each of you one very important question. Are you prepared to receive a—' He stood up and turned to face the audience. '—Custard pie in the face?'

The crowd cheered. The three kids cheered. The girl jumped up and down, making her pigtails bounce, and shouted, 'Me! Oh! Me!' I liked her right away. She acted like a younger me.

Cowardy Custard reached into the cabinet. He produced a small velvet sack, a paper plate and a tube of whipped cream. He filled the plate with heaps of cream. On his return to the children he tripped again, threatening to press the custard pie into his own face. The crowd bellowed.

'Let's get the rules straight,' he said, holding up the sack. 'In this bag there are four ribbons—three yellow and one red. We're going to take it in turns to pull out a ribbon. Pick a yellow and you're safe. Pick the red one, though...' He brandished the paper plate with its shuddering pile of cream. 'And you'll get a custard pie in the face!'

The children in the crowd roared. The two volunteer boys now looked pale and uncertain. The girl hopped up and down, still shouting, 'Me!'

'I'll need somebody trustworthy to make sure I play fair,' Cowardy Custard said. He pointed at dad. 'We know we can trust this man, don't we?'

By this point I started to wonder if dad might be in on the whole thing. Perhaps he knew the magician? But if that was the case, dad put on a good show. With a display of reluctance, he stepped over the rope barrier. He balked when the magician handed him the plate of whipped cream. I heard him whisper, 'You're really going to make me throw a custard pie at a kid?'

The magician grinned and raised his voice so that everyone could hear. 'Rather you be the bad guy than me!'

Everybody laughed.

I watched dad's face. He looked suspicious, and not just for show. He glanced at me and winked, then zipped up his hoodie so that it covered his checked shirt entirely.

'Let's get this show on the road! I'll let you go first,' Cowardy Custard said to the shortest boy.

The boy put his hand into the sack. He pulled out a yellow ribbon. He grinned.

'Lucky, lucky!' the magician said. He turned to my dad. 'We won't be needing you just yet, sir!'

Dad acted like he was limbering up his throwing arm. The crowd loved it.

The next boy took his turn. He winced as he reached into the sack. Another yellow ribbon.

Cowardy Custard bent down to the girl. 'Just you and me left, then! How do you fancy your chances?'

The girl hadn't stopped jumping up and down. She presented her face to my dad, inviting the custard pie.

'Hold your horses,' the magician said. 'We haven't even chosen our ribbons yet. Do you want to pick one, or do you want me to pick one?'

'You!' the girl said.

The magician gave my dad a subtle thumbs-up. He took his time reaching into the sack. 'It's a...' He pulled out a red ribbon, held it up for all to see, then jammed it back into the bag. 'Yellow ribbon!'

The children in the crowd booed.

'Cheat!' one of the parents shouted.

Cowardy Custard made a 'who me?' face.

The girl hopped up and down.

My dad frowned. He'd been watching the girl, not the magician. He kept blinking, fast. Now he saw that Cowardy Custard held a yellow ribbon. He looked at the magician for reassurance. The magician beamed and nodded.

'Boys and girls!' Cowardy Custard shouted. 'Who do you think deserves a custard pie in the face?'

'The big cheat!' somebody called out.

The suggestions of the crowd became an unintelligible clamour. Most children pointed at the magician, though not all of them. Dad seemed even more confused. He mouthed a question.

'It's your call,' the magician said to him. He leant forwards and closed his eyes.

Dad shoved the custard pie into the six-year-old girl's face.

The entire crowd was silent. The only sound was an excited squeak from the little girl, who still danced around. Whipped cream dropped from her face and onto her dress and shoes.

Parents behind the rope barrier began to mutter.

Cowardy Custard stared at my dad.

Dad stared at the girl.

After a few frozen seconds, the magician bent down. He helped to clear cream from the girl's eyes.

'I'm so sorry,' he said. 'Are you okay?'

The girl had stopped laughing. Now that she could see again she gazed out at the audience. Perhaps she was searching for her parents. I looked around too. The children around me didn't know quite what to make of it all. The adults were wide-eyed and concerned.

Once she registered the disbelief from the crowd, the girl began to cry.

Cowardy Custard finished up the show as best he could. He stammered and tripped up, for real.

At the rear of the tent, dad dabbed at the girl's face with a towel. His hands shook. She cried and cried.

It wasn't until after the show had finished and the crowds had wandered away that the girl's parents appeared. A slim, pretty woman pushed past my dad to take over towelling duties. The girl's father took one look at dad, then threw a punch.

Dad hadn't wanted to talk about it, and I didn't question it. I guess he must have told mum, back home, must have had to explain the bruise under his eye. In the way that seven, maybe eight-year-olds do, I conflated this event and several others. Now, when I look back, the Cowardy Custard incident was the moment when things started to go bad, culminating in dad leaving home three months later and never showing up again. It all made sense enough to me. That day, Dad had made a bad judgement, which hinted at other bad judgements. And that day, I lost my faith in him.

An Intervention

by

Andreina Cordani

I know, officer, it's most irregular isn't it? I can understand why you'd want to check it out. After all, when you find someone handcuffed to a lamp post wearing a gorilla suit it's usually a man, right? Some poor sod of a stag with over-enthusiastic mates. I bet you didn't expect to lift that ape mask and find the respected finance director of an international company.

Yes, that's me. No, I don't have any ID. Does this thing look like it has pockets?

I'm sure we can get this cleared up relatively quickly. I'm happy to explain.

You know how it is, when you lose touch with old friends from uni. The past few years have been so busy with work and of course with meeting Jared, the amazing love of my life, that I lost track. But when Jared proposed I knew I wanted Lish, Sam and Ellen to be my bridesmaids.

I took them all out for Champagne to announce it. It was lovely to see them – they really hadn't changed a bit over the last three years. Ellen was still a teacher, Lish dabbled in theatre and lived off her parents and Sam had done the mum thing – she looked two stone heavier and very tired.

'I don't want it to be an overblown wedding,' I told them. 'Just a simple, beautiful day with a laid back vibe.'

Then I handed out the spreadsheets.

As I talked them through the plans, with each of their roles highlighted in a different colour, I

noticed them all looking at me, and at each other.

'Is there a problem?' I asked, genuinely worried I'd missed something out.

The three of them shook their heads. 'You really have it all planned out, don't you?' said Ellen admiringly. I smiled at the compliment. I've always believed that whatever you want in life you can make it happen; you just need to focus and stay in control.

We met several times for 'bridal board meetings' where I checked on everyone's progress. And I admit I was sometimes a little firm with them, but you have to be straight when you want to get the job done. And I helped them out in return – I even hooked Sam up with a diet service that sends healthy food to your door and provides exercise and counselling so you can keep the weight off.

To be honest, I wanted to get her back into a size 12 as the frocks don't come any bigger – but I had her best interests at heart. And she was doing so well until this weekend.

Ah yes, this weekend.

I wanted a hen night that fit perfectly with the homespun theme of my wedding. No feather boas and fluffy handcuffs for me. There's a beautiful little town just down the coast from here – do you know it? The police are probably a lot less busy down there – you might want to consider a transfer.

Anyway, I found I found a bunting workshop and pottery course and thought it would be a great idea to hand-make the plates for the top table – I've never seen that at a wedding before. Don't you think it's a lovely idea? Well, I do.

I know it's the chief bridesmaid's duty to organise these things, so I fired off an email to Lish and the girls with a schedule and costings attached.

They took a little longer than I expected to reply but just as I started to panic Lish got back to me and said it was all booked. We'd go in Ellen's camper van, she said, so we could all drive down together.

I pictured us all travelling down in one of those classic VW campers – probably in duck egg blue with cheery bunting in the windows. But what pulled up outside my flat was a 1970s monstrosity with orange swirly curtains. Half of it was held together with duct tape.

Ellen was at the wheel, Lish and Sam had their faces pressed up against the glass, wearing pink flashing headbands, brandishing an open bottle of Cava and a set of fluffy handcuffs. I groaned to myself – what part of 'no tacky stuff' did they not understand?

'Let the henning begin,' Lish said, thrusting a plastic Champagne flute into my hand. Now, I'm not a big fan of Cava, and I'd hoped to spend some of the journey crocheting little lace doilies for the guests' tables. But the van was far too bumpy for that and I was threatened with the cuffs if I didn't drink. I hadn't had more than half a glass of red in months and I got drunk shamefully easily.

By the time I realised we were coming into Bournemouth I was feeling a bit blurry at the edges. Ellen agreed we must have taken a wrong turn, but we drove through the darkening streets for what seemed like hours, with Lish holding up her phone to get satnav reception.

Then suddenly the van engine gave a little cough and died.

Ellen let out a groan and said something like 'I knew this would happen.'

Fighting to sober up I staggered out with the others to peer pointlessly under the hood. As I listened to Ellen and Sam bicker about whether the left trunnion had blown there was a tap on my shoulder, and a voice said, 'can we be of assistance?'

It's not often that a girl turns round to find a policeman a fireman and a doctor looking at her. Through the fog of Cava my common sense told me it was fancy dress, but for a moment it felt as if all my emergency services had come at once.

You see I've always had a bit of a uniform thing. The girls used to tease me about it at college – I went out with so many paramedics and firemen, and as for policemen, well...

Ahem. Moving on.

So it turned out these guys worked at a nearby bar, Dreamboiz, and they invited us inside for a drink while Ellen waited for the RAC. No, don't feel sorry for her – you'll find out later why she doesn't deserve it.

This next part I'm not proud of: When we got inside, I made a decision. I hadn't planned a hen night in Bournemouth, but I was here, there were cocktails, male strippers and loud music. So I went with it.

I drank. I laughed. The guys danced and I threw £20 notes at them. Sam downed about fifteen Baileys cocktails – I could practically see the pounds go back on. We talked about all the stupid stuff we did at uni – Lish's kleptomaniac phase, Ellen's disastrous relationship with Spliffy Pete the dealer, and the time I brought a date to one of Pete's parties forgetting he was a policeman.

We'll leave that part out of the statement, if you don't mind.

As the night wore on, we even went backstage and played cards with the guys. Have you ever played strip poker with a stripper? You have? Well you know they cheat, then. Within half an hour my clothes were scattered around the room and I was down to my bra and pants. The only person wearing less than me was Gary the Gorilla, and that's just because his suit is an all-in-one.

Anyway, it was fun. All that wedding crap melted away and I realised that's what hen nights are for. To remind you who you are, and make sure that even if you change a little (and you have to, if you want to be a finance director) you don't change too much. 'I love you lot,' I told my friends. 'And that's not just the cocktails talking.'

Gary made a slightly camp little *aaaww* face at me. 'So you liked your hen night surprise then?' he said. 'When Lish rang I wasn't sure she could pull it off but it really worked, didn't it? You were a bit up yourself when you got here, but now look at you...'

Everyone in the room froze, but Gary was prattling on about how he and Lish were old acting buddies, how he and the boys had been more than happy to help out after our 'little breakdown'.

The air around me was completely still but I felt hot, my chest thudded as the realisation came crashing in. They'd lied to me, they'd moaned about me behind my back, called me uptight, boring... *I thought they were my friends.*

I had to get out, barked at someone to give me my clothes. With a snigger, one of the strippers threw Gary's gorilla suit at me.

Fine. Be like that.

I rushed to the ladies' and scrambled into the suit. It was sticky and pungent but I didn't care. Outside the chilly night air gave me energy. I heard the girls' voices behind me and broke into a run.

Ellen was the first to catch up – I shouted at her to go away, but instead she grabbed me. Her hands were like iron round my wrists and within seconds I was chained to that lamp post by the fluffy cuffs.

The other girls caught up now. Lish was carrying a satin G string, a Dreamboiz shot glass and the gorilla mask (Like I said: kleptomaniac.) Sam had to go off to one side to be sick.

'We tried talking to you,' Ellen said. 'At every one of those terrible, boring bridal board meetings we wanted to say something. But you're so difficult to talk to.'

Sam dabbed at her mouth with a tissue. 'You were changing, you weren't you any more.'

'So...' Lish said, out of breath but also milking the situation for drama, 'this is an intervention.'

They laid it all out in front of me. How I'd disappeared from their lives, how I'd never even met Sam's daughter, how I'd bullied and scheduled them until the wedding didn't feel like fun at all. I could feel the tears coming but I don't do tears – I prefer anger.

I turned on them. How could they be so ungrateful? All those diet meals I'd bought for Sam, the couture dresses I was spending a fortune on so they weren't stuck with aubergine meringues. And what was wrong with being driven? At least I'd done something with my life, I had the flat, the car, built an amazing career – not like their sad little lives...

It took me a couple of seconds for my brain to catch up with what I'd said. Their faces were blank with shock.

Ellen was the first to recover – her lips a thin line, the way teachers always look when they're controlling their anger. 'We're going to get a coffee,' she said. 'You can wait here and sober up.'

Solemnly, Lish put the gorilla mask over my head. Through the eyeholes, I watched them walk away.

The moment they left, all my anger drained out of me and then the tears did come. Hidden inside the mask it didn't seem to matter and I let myself cry it out. Was I really such an unapproachable control-freak that they had to do all this to avoid an awkward chat?

The mask was stuffy and steamy with sweat and tears. I sobbed and gulped and then just leant against the lamp post in exhaustion. I no longer cared that there would be no handmade china at the wedding, or that Sam was never going to get into that dress. But the thought of getting married without them there made me feel crumpled, small and lonely.

Anyway, that's when you found me. I must say I was lucky you came along so soon after they left. Actually, maybe you got here *too* quickly... Hang on a minute... What an idiot I've been! You're another stripper, aren't you?

Aren't you?

OK, my mistake. That does look like a real warrant card, officer.

Do you think it'll take long to process me? I'd like to get going now. I have to find my friends and apologise. If we can find a hotel and grab a few hours sleep we might still make it to the pottery class on time tomorrow.

Oh yes, of course we're still going, we have a schedule. But there might be some Cava involved too.

Small Talk

by

Charlotte Brazier

There were two words that struck fear into the very heart of Arthur Beswick.

They were not *tax return*, *no signal* or *prostate exam*, but *small talk*.

The very thought of making inane chit-chat was enough to make him writhe in bed each Sunday night, the mental images of his colleagues asking how his weekend was strangling him like the tentacles of Medusa.

It was not that Arthur was unfriendly: quite the opposite. He loved to talk. He loved to talk about books and space and foreign affairs and travel and cooking and films and music. He loved to ask questions and learn new facts. But most people didn't want to talk about those things, and Arthur couldn't think of the words to join in with their conversations. It was like all of the words had been vacuumed right out of his brain.

Despite his colleagues' belligerent attempts to crack him open like the top of a crème brûlée, he shied away from idle chat and his monosyllabic responses punctuated the conversation like the staccato of a Tchaikovsky prelude.

Arthur supposed that some people's brains were wired for small talk and his brain was wired for other things, like poetry and playing the piano and compiling lists and parallel parking. He didn't think there was anything wrong with not wanting to waste time talking about rubbish. It seemed unfair that it was acceptable to put the phone down on someone talking about double glazing but it was rude to walk away from someone who was telling boring anecdotes about their children.

He was happy by himself, and very rarely felt lonely. When he was on his own in his poky little flat, he could concentrate and all of his thoughts buzzed around in his head until it wasn't quiet anymore.

Arthur's flat was perfectly functional. His clothes were organised by both sleeve length and texture so if there was ever a power cut he could find his clothes in the dark. The bathroom was spotless, each of the shampoo labels facing forwards. His shelves were lined with all of the classics: *Dr Jekyll and Mr Hyde, To Kill a Mockingbird* and *The Bell Jar*.

Arthur liked books. He liked that if you had enough of someone, you could close the book and put them back on the shelf. You couldn't do that in real life.

Standing at an impressive 6ft 2in with thick brown hair, Arthur was an attractive man. He kept his body sinewy by completing weight exercises in his bedroom each morning, and he had soft tendrils of hair on his 32-year-old chest that he concealed beneath a crisp white shirt. If he had been a character in a book, Arthur believed the author would have written that he had sexual allure.

Arthur had worked as an IT consultant at SmallTech Trade for the last eighteen months and twelve days. He had been in love with Melanie from accounts for the last eighteen months and four days, and he thought perhaps she loved him too. She put a smiley face on his wage slip and he knew she didn't put a smiley face on anyone else's wage slip because he had checked.

Arthur knew he was in love because Melanie made his heart flutter and his hands clammy and he wanted to protect her. He was going to tell her all that tonight, at 5.30pm.

It was currently 5.20pm and Arthur was getting nervous. He had never told a woman that he loved her before, and he wasn't quite sure how to go about it. If this had been a book, he would have galloped in on a noble steed or whisked her away to a tropical paradise or spelt it out using candles. But this was not a book, and he didn't have any candles.

At 5.21pm, their boss, Mr King, called everyone into the office. Arthur knew that Mr King was cross because his face was all crumpled up like a crisp packet that has been trodden on. He was waving his hands and shouting about mistakes and although Arthur knew that he wasn't shouting at him because he didn't make mistakes, Arthur didn't like it.

Mr King stopped waving his arms and looked at Arthur. He peered into his eyes and Arthur peered back until he felt it had been a terribly long time so he looked at the whiteboard instead. Arthur suspected that Mr King thought he was strange, but everybody seemed to think he was strange so it did not offend him.

Arthur wished Mr King would stop talking because he needed to take some books back to the library by 6pm or he would get fined and it was already 5.26pm and it was a 24-minute walk to the library which gave him only 10 minutes spare and he still had to tell Melanie that he loved her and he didn't know how long that would take.

Melanie was sat quietly by the window, her big green eyes focused on Mr King. She had long, elegant fingers that were tearing paper into shreds that littered her desk like snowflakes. With her curly red hair and freckled nose, Arthur thought Melanie was the most beautiful woman he had ever seen.

A phone cried shrilly, like a pterodactyl about to attack. Mr King picked it up and spoke into the receiver before gesturing impatiently for them all to leave.

As everyone else filed out of the room, Arthur waited in his seat and watched Melanie sweep up the snowflakes and sprinkle them into the wastepaper basket. She grabbed her handbag and walked past Arthur, down the corridor and into the kitchen. Taking a deep breath, Arthur picked up his mug and followed her inside.

He closed the kitchen door behind them and set his mug on the counter before spinning to face her.

'Melanie, your hair is like the flames of a fire, your eyes like precious stones. I have watched you for eighteen months and twelve days now, and I believe that I would make you happy. I am kind, considerate and computer literate. I earn a good wage and I can cook, clean and complete basic DIY tasks. Would you like to go on a date with me? I am free on Monday, Tuesday, Wednesday, Friday, Saturday and Sunday but not on Thursday because I have badminton.'

Melanie, with her eyes like precious stones, looked at him curiously..

'Yep,' she said.

Keep Them Rollin'

by

Rosanne Rabinowitz

'You are making history,' they told us at our 'Motivating the Motivators' course. 'You're part of the great reformation of the British welfare system!'

But my cubicle in the open-plan office doesn't look like a history-making room. No maps with pins and flags adorn my partition, only a generic landscape painting of cliffs and waves and appropriately humble fisherfolk. It's hanging crooked, for some reason, so I put it straight just as my first 'customer' arrives.

Middle-aged lady, faded 1990s rock-chick look. Kitted out like she's off to a gig rather than an interview. Hoodie, t-shirt with an unreadable name on it. Denim skirt, black leggings, trainers. About my age and my height, but bulkier, with a battered cardboard folder under her arm. She sits down before I invite her, and places her folder on her lap.

Presentation skills need work. I make a mental note as I smile at her. 'You must be Wendy Smith. I'll just get your file up on the computer.'

The screen comes to life, and the desktop icons dance in front of me. I rub my eyes. I'm having trouble finding Wendy Smith's file. Could I really be hungover from last night? It was just a few drinks with Miriam from IT.

No, it's the damn system playing up again. No surprise after five years of constant overhauls, write-offs and restarts from scratch.

Whole thing's so cocked up they've just brought in another new bunch of experts, Miriam says. It's all about 'quantum computing' now.

So it's a big thing, this quantum computing. Government put millions into it. 'All theoretical,' Miriam said last night. She does like to bend my ear, and she likes a drink too. Must be all the stress they get in IT.

'But they're getting practical real fast around here. A universal computer system for Universal Credit! Or shall we say *multiversal*, Gwen?' She downed the last of her drink with a chuckle.

I didn't quite see the humour. 'Call it what you want, it sounds like gobbledygook to me.' Then I went to the bar for more G&Ts.

Miriam carried on talking shop, but after a few drinks it was sounding more and more like a shop located on another planet.

At last, there's the profile for Wendy Smith, who shares my run-of-the-mill surname. Blimey. Where did she get that haircut, in a poodle parlour? I also notice the date of birth. Same as mine. Just goes to show what a crock astrology is.

I take my time before I speak. Silence makes people squirm, ready to spill.

'So Wendy, we need to talk about your Claimant Commitment, which will set out what you must do in return for our help. We have your tax records, but we need to know more since you've not been on the Job Centre system before.'

'Maybe it's because I already have a job. Two of them.'

Wendy speaks with a smile, so 'firm but polite'. Bet she'll talk about 'rights' next.

Expect that from working claimants, we were told at training. So now it's time to initiate a 'challenging conversation'.

I turn up my own smile. 'Now we have a new system, so just having a job is not enough. We ask you to try to progress in your work and increase your earnings, and provide proof of that. To get started, why don't you tell me more about what you do.'

She looks at me like I'm an insect that just buzzed in, and grips that thick folder on her lap as if she'd love to swat me with it.

'I'm a freelance editor and writer,' she finally says.

'That must be lovely! But you're still not earning enough to support yourself without claiming in-work benefits. And that's what we have to tackle.'

She nods. 'OK, let's do that. I was fine on my income ten, even five years ago. But my rent has doubled since then. And the publishers have cut their rates.'

I beam her my 'tough but sympathetic' look. This is accomplished by a steady stare, keeping eye contact but giving the lips a faint upward twitch.

'But Wendy, we have to move on. It's up to *you* to make the changes you want, and not blame anyone or anything else for shortcomings.'

A burst of laughter greets that motivating morsel. 'Oh yeah, and I bet 'there's no such thing as society,' like your hero Margaret Thatcher said.'

'That's quite an assumption...' I begin. Then I see she's looking at the painting behind me.

'Those cows look like they were made by a cookie-cutter,' she says. 'No perspective. Where'd you get that thing?'

Cows? I look over my shoulder. The sea and the cliffs have been replaced by rolling hills and... badly painted cows, splotched with greasy-looking patches of purple. That picture has *changed*. Who? When? My mind refuses to accept it; my stomach lurches.

But I'm a professional and I will continue this interview.

I turn away from the painting. 'You weren't invited here to comment on cows. We need to talk about your responsibilities as a claimant, and your work.'

'So I have some queries, all about my work!' She takes a sheaf of papers from her folder. 'These are documents produced by your office. *Universal Credit at Work, Guidance for Work Coaches*... from the Freedom of Information Act and all that.'

She displays a page peppered with words circled in red. 'Drive' must be used fifteen times here. Drive earnings progression, drive the attitudes of low-earning claimants, driving a step-change in behaviours... *Drive, drive, drive. Are you talking about cattle or sheep? Keep those dogies rollin', rollin rollin rollin...*'

Is she singing 'Rawhide'? Indie bands did ironic covers of that song many years ago when I didn't do much work myself and spent too much time at festivals. I can hear that music now, coming from the main stage while I was waiting in queue to use the satellite phone... A festival in Cornwall where everyone was off their faces and the portaloos overflowed with shit.

Wendy points at another red-circled word. 'Incentivize? Spelt with 'z', no less.' She shudders. 'Do you know what one of my editors said? Any writer using 'incentivize' should be taken out and shot.' She lifts her hand in a 'stop' gesture. 'Not that I'm advocating *that*. But really... How can an organisation that produces such bad writing and churns out such swill be entitled to tell me how to do my job? Incentivise this, incentivise that! Sounds like a bloody Dalek. *Incentivise! Incentivise!*'

Though she hasn't raised her voice, people are looking at us. Dalek-speak carries. Daleks! But last night Miriam was also talking rubbish straight out of Doctor Who as she rambled on about quantum computing. Qubits in many places at the same time, and people who might do that too. Parallel universes.

'*Incentivise!*' There she goes again.

Stay professional. Just remember I'm in control. Others have power over me – like that tight-arsed area manager – but I still decide what happens here.

I take a breath and modulate my tones to express patience and forbearance. 'If you keep creating a disturbance, I'll have to ask you to leave.'

The computer emits a clickety-click. I'm still afraid to look at that painting.

'But I'm being perfectly reasonable,' Wendy protests. 'And I have nothing against you personally. I know you have such a tough job.' Concern knits her brows, and her face flushes with faux sympathy. Same face I put on as I pretend to 'help' while I'm really shoehorning some loser onto a scheme with a multimillion pound contract.

In fact, there are seconds when Wendy could be me... wearing a fright-wig. I pat my short hair for reassurance.

'You know, I almost went to work at the Job Centre myself.' she says. 'When I applied, I thought I'd go 'undercover' and help people get their money. But I'd already arranged to go to a festival, so I planned to ring my flatmates to find out about interviews. When I was queuing at the phone stall a friend walked by and said hey, come see a band. I thought, sod this. And when I got home a week later I found a letter saying I had an interview, but I'd missed it.'

'So you missed a job interview?' I make a note.

'Yeah? So that was in 1989,' she laughs. 'Even if your sanctioning schtick does go retroactive, it couldn't extend that far back.'

The queasy feeling returns as I remember. I'm waiting among the stalls selling overpriced veggie burgers and hippie tat. I'm anxious to make my phone call. If I have an interview I'll leave. I won't stay for the rest of the festival or join friends on a trip to St Just.

'Was... Was the festival in Cornwall?' My voice sounds distant in my ears. 'Was there a band on the main stage playing 'Rawhide'?'

'Yes! Were you there? It was a *mental*, that festival! And the loos were disgusting. But I had a good time in the end...'

Rollin' rollin' rollin', keep 'em rollin' rollin'. No, I told my friends. I've been waiting too long to give up on my phone call.

The receptionist comes by my partition. 'Gwen! Your next customer is here.'

Snap out of it, snap snap snap!

I'm tempted to wave Wendy on her way after ticking the right boxes. Why argue, when I can fulfil goals with more tractable and less mouthy individuals?

And she reminds of times I've forgotten – or tried to forget. Moments that didn't involve shit or squalor. Finding a stage far into the woods, bands playing on it, creating music I hadn't heard before and haven't heard since.

'Customer...' Wendy is saying. 'When I last signed on, no one called us *customers*.'

Two bands jamming, creating a weave of sound that will never exist again. I could have slipped out of the queue. To hear more, I could have become like the woman in front of me. I could be living in chaos, too.

The computer's gone to sleep. I have to log on again. The document materialises, but the text has turned into hieroglyphics. A vortex forms in the middle of the screen. But it dissipates and there's Wendy Smith's profile at last. With short hair.

That's not Wendy Smith. It's me.

Or both of us. Our images are layered, mingling in the same space. Wendy, Gwen, both. My stomach starts knotting again, the ground pitching under my feet.

'Different probabilities, and a computer that can calculate them.' Miriam was truly sloshed and slurring by last orders. 'So quantum computing's gonna save Universal Credit. That's what they *say*. But maybe they want to influence claimant behaviour! Imagine different versions of each claimant in many universes, living out different decisions. Maybe there's one who isn't unemployed?'

I close my eyes. Open them again to look at the real and rather cross Wendy Smith.

'What are you doing? Did you really write about my missed interview in 1989? But I did get work in publishing later.'

'And look where you are now,' I remind her.

'Yeah... it could be worse.' Wendy waves, indicating the vast strip-lit room around us... security guards at the door, tense talk as people are interrogated. Sobbing from the reception area. That better not be my next customer

And Wendy is looking at me. It could be worse.

That's it. 'I'm afraid our time's up,' I say. 'I'll write to you about our next appointment.'

Wendy can't get out fast enough, papers trailing behind her. She turns to give an exaggerated salute.

Bitch. But she was right about one thing. We can't sanction claimants for actions before their claim. Yet. However, I can flag up her comments as suggesting an entrenched aversion to work. That justifies a sanction, in addition to disrupting our interview. Six months of no benefit? With her rent she'll feel the pinch.

Then I book her for a four-week programme with Grow Aspiration Success, the same organisation that ran our training. She'll enjoy the full battery of neurolinguistic programming and mind-melding techniques.

And at last I do get around to ticking the box: 'refer to decision-maker.' *Sanctioned*.

Moments in Time

by

Tom Hunter

Later I would say that the single best moment of our school exchange trip to Germany was the moment when the airplane depressurised.

Trapped in a window seat, surrounded by panicked classmates scratching at the overhead panels for their oxygen masks, I just did my best to ignore it all.

I was on the last chapter of my new book, and I really wanted to find out how everything ended before we hit the ground.

Reading was a camouflage that I had relied on to keep me alive and relatively unnoticed all through the long week of the exchange programme. A class of fourteen-year-olds bound together for a week in Stadtallendorf, a small town in what our teachers told us was called the West Hesse Depression Zone. Apparently named for its low and rolling geography, but I had my suspicions about that one.

David Bowie recorded my favourite of his albums in Germany, starting with Low, which is probably all the information you need to form a pretty accurate impression of me as a teenager. I doubt even the Thin White Duke himself could have found much to amuse and inspire in the West Hesse DZ though: a place still enthusiastically embracing the worst of the 80s as we finally turned the corner into the next decade.

Then again, I doubt many parents would have signed off on a cultural exchange trip if our teachers had proposed a greatest hits tour of Bowie's Berlin.

My parents could never understand why my language skills were always so terrible. I lived in books after all, but that was literature, not language, and I'd always seemed to miss the classes that covered the basics of communication – vowels, verbs, past-participles and so on – and skipped straight to the storytelling.

By the time I was introduced to the existence of masculine and feminine nouns and the whole concept of compound-complex sentences, the battle was already lost. Whatever plasticity my brain might have begun with had long since settled into fixed grooves of passive resistance; a defensive shield entirely capable of deflecting the invasive influence of any alien tongues.

I was a fourteen-year-old boy who found almost all conversation difficult, and my chosen exchange partner, Nils, showed no interest in acknowledging me at all, let alone sharing the secrets of his language.

Nils Hansa. My cultural nemesis in double denim and Hi-Tecs. Sixteen years old, a foot taller than me and loaded with export-strength testosterone.

Our unthinking teachers had twinned us with a school group two whole years older than us, a cultural age gap that stretched wider than the ice ages that once ground out Stadtallendorf's depressed basins and valleys.

The German girls took this in their stride, uniformly adopting their partners as temporary younger sisters, but for the boys our younger age was another unwelcome layer of conversation that needed to be navigated and a difficult reminder that they were closer to us than the adults we all pretended to be.

'Diesel,' Nils said, putting a pint down in front of me.

Nils might have liked to think he looked old enough to get served anywhere, but he and his friends still hung out exclusively in the local youth club rather than any of the nearby bars, even though they wanted us to believe this was all by personal choice.

I was there because Nils was there, and Nils was tasked to look after me when all the official school tours and language coaching had finished for the day.

None of his friends were on the exchange programme, which made our one shared connection the fact we'd both been co-opted into this week by our parents, but that didn't stop him acting as though everything were somehow my fault, which sort of explained the pint of Diesel.

Nils rode a dirt bike.

Nils carried a folding knife.

Nils drank Diesel.

Never mind that Diesel was basically a lager shandy made with some kind of cheap, flat coke rather than lemonade and tasted absolutely disgusting. Also, it was the only alcoholic drink available in the youth club.

Nils and his crew chugged at their pints while I sipped at mine and wondered if they'd care if I started reading my latest book while they played out their endless rounds on the pool table.

Reading at the speed of life.

A recorded voice demands my attention: 'The aircraft cabin is depressurising. Please fasten oxygen mask securely over your nose and mouth and remain seated.'

Only no oxygen masks are being released from overhead and everyone around me is freaking out.

I do my best to make it fade away.

I must not fear. Fear is the mind-killer, says the reluctant hero of my book as he prepares to fight for his life.

I'm three pages from reaching the end of my book, and the galactic wars and duels and intrigues are almost done.

I feel sicker inside than I did after my fifth pint of Diesel, but I turn the page.

Two to go.

It's 2am and I'm doing my best to vomit quietly.

Diesel may be weak but I'm weaker, and I don't want to give Nils the satisfaction.

There's a knock on the bathroom door, so soft I almost miss it. I don't want to unlock it at first, but the voice whispering at me isn't my exchange partner. It's his sister, Emerly.

Emerly Hansa. Younger sister of my nemesis and so far almost invisible throughout the duration of my visit. Thirteen years old and gangly where her brother is all bulk, but still almost a foot taller than me.

She's sitting with her knees tucked up under her chin so I can sit on the other end of her bed with as much distance between us as possible. I'm on my third glass of water, and we haven't spoken so much as gestured silently at each other and shared one brief moment of contact when she took my hand and led me into her bedroom.

Nils had grudging told me that, despite their three-year age gap, his sister was already scoring higher than him in written language classes, but that she barely spoke to people in German, let alone English, and he doubted I'd see her much, let alone hear her.

He told me this while lifting me off the ground and swinging me around upside down in the car park outside the youth club, the night I first arrived in Stadtallendorf.

Physical superiority established and friends amused, I understood better than Nils that the rationale for this particular humiliation was to demonstrate his belief that brute strength would always win out over any facility with syntax or simile.

Sat on the edge of her bed, I appreciated the irony that Emerly and I were still proving Nils' theory by relying on our body language and the frisson of a shared enemy to bridge the gaps in our communication.

In a letter, years later, Emerly told me how she once stole the manual for Nils' dirt bike and worked out the best ways to fudge the engine, brakes and fuel line so that he was always stalling on the track and losing races.

'I even told him once that his bike sounded funny and what the problem was,' she wrote, 'but he ignored me like he always does. I learnt a lesson, he kept on losing, and the next time I took twice as many pieces from the bike.'

Inside the envelope was a dull metal bolt that still smelt faintly of burnt engine oil.

'The aircraft cabin is depressurising...'

The teachers are shouting for everyone to stay calm.

'Please fasten oxygen mask securely over your nose and mouth and remain seated.'

There are no masks. The overhead panels are still sealed tight, and I think I can smell something burning.

'The aircraft cabin is depressurising...'

I admit I'm skim-reading now, but I'm down to the final page.

Emerly and I waited together in silence. What we were waiting for, I couldn't tell you. Only that we were suspended in our own moment in time, Emerly waiting on me and me waiting on her.

The lights were off, but I felt too wrung out to sleep. Besides I could sense her watching me, an odd mixture of calm concern and wry amusement in her shadowed posture, and her hand on an old plastic salad bowl, ready should I have another emergency.

I came to believe Emerly somehow understood me completely. That she could see inside me, read my mind, even share her thoughts with me so they hung like pictures glowing in the dark space between us.

Some people wait their whole lives before they learn how to share a silence. Longer still before they come to enjoy it. Leaving words unsaid can be more difficult than any conversation, and no matter what we say, we all want our own moment to be heard.

Emerly told me later, in her first letter, that she'd only come to check on me as part of her on-going revenge campaign against Nils. That helping me avoid a humiliating hangover would weaken his macho posture and maybe he'd become bored enough to let me survive the next few days until I could get back on a plane.

And then she'd seen how difficult I found it to speak to her, even though she could have replied easily enough with no else watching or judging and given time to write the sentences out in her head first before speaking.

Instead she'd stayed quiet, and I'd stayed quiet, and the longer the moment lasted the less she wanted to break it.

I woke up the next morning alone and still propped up against her bedroom wall, the sound of Nils' dirt bike revving from the driveway outside.

At some point she must have removed the glass of water I'd balanced in my lap for fear I'd spill it in my sleep, and instead she's replaced it with a thick paperback book and a note that said:

It's in English.
You came into my room to borrow it.
It's still too difficult for me.
You can keep it if you like.
E.

THE END.

I reach the last sentence in Emerly's book and look up from the page to see my classmates sat in silent, almost unnatural calm all around me.

'... short circuit in our recorded message system, but there's nothing to worry about.'

At the end of the aisle a stewardess with a drinks trolley hands my teacher what looks like a tiny plastic glass of Diesel.

'Again, the aircraft is completely secure, and as a gesture of goodwill on behalf of the airline the cabin crew will be distributing additional drinks and snacks to everyone for the duration of the journey.'

No actual loss of pressure. No oxygen masks needed. No burning. Just a glitch in the electronics that plays our aeroplane's automatic messages and a moment in time when everyone on board thought it was really the end.

'Thank you, and please enjoy the rest of your flight.'

I stay quiet, of course, but inside I'm laughing. Almost the end of the world, and of course I hide in a book.

I turn back the pages and reread the ending again properly.

After that, I take out my exercise book and start my first letter to Emerly.

A Gift

by

Adam Smith

'Happy birthday, Cara. There's something I must tell you, but I need you to know that your mother loves you the same no matter what.'

She stopped in the middle of the kitchen and turned to look at me. Sixteen today, in black leggings and a washed out T-shirt that said Jesus Is My Home Boy.

'Do we have to do this now?'

Her green eyes blinked in the afternoon light, like they did on the day she was born. They looked the same, save for the dark rings she'd painted around them.

'Sit with me a moment, please.' I watched her eyebrows draw together like a child's drawing of a bird.

'Can't this wait? My friends will be here soon.'

As I pulled out a chair for her to sit down, the doorbell rang. She turned on her heels, smiling over her shoulder as she left the room. Sixteen today. She was used to getting her own way.

I heard her look through the spy hole and adjust her expression before she opened the door.

'Aunt Chloe.'

'Happy birthday darling. I've got something bubbly for you. Don't tell your father.'

Chloe popped the cork, white foam fizzing over her hands and onto the grass. She poured drinks for Cara and her friends. They raised their glasses in a toast. Cara tossed her hair over her shoulder as she sipped her Prosecco, acting like she'd never tasted alcohol before.

I sat with Laura in the shade of an umbrella. 'Would you like any cake?' I asked. She blinked twice for no. I watched an ant crawl across the uneaten birthday cake, pulling its little black body over the white icing.

'Cara, come over here,' I said. She rolled her eyes for her friends and drained her glass. 'Your mother has something she would like to give you.'

53

The matte had rubbed off the ring so it was shinier than the day I proposed. I thought about the way the dust had glowed as the light came through the doors of the registry office that day. Laura in a long white gown, still walking unaided. Chloe next to her in a tight purple dress. You'd never guess they were sisters if it wasn't for their hair; shocking tendrils of red which fell over their shoulders.

Cara had the same hair, I watched it bounce as she walked towards us. She was as tall as Chloe, not short like Laura. 'Our little girl, all grown up,' I said to Laura. 'Doesn't she look great'.

Laura blinked once for yes.

'This is your mother's engagement ring,' I told Cara. 'Now you're sixteen she would like to give it to you.'.

'But I can't take this.' Cara's eyes were wet, and in her expression I saw compassion, love and something else. Something hungry.

'Of course you can,' I said. 'It will make your mother very happy.'

The ring was cold and smooth against my open palm. She took it a little too fast, slipped it onto her middle finger, then held her hand flat so she could see how it looked. 'I love it,' she bent down to hug Laura, I watched Laura's head roll as Cara's shoulder pressed into her neck brace.

The word hereditary screamed through my brain, but I shook it away and forced a smile.

The shadow of the gazebo looked like a wounded animal sprawling on the lawn, Cara sat cross-legged beside a pile of presents. She opened them one by one, her friends clapping and squealing as she pulled away the paper.

I thought about the gifts we'd brought her over the years: leotards, Sea Monkeys, the doll that shit its pants,

Sparks the hamster. He was buried in the flowerbed a few yards from where she sat.

I turned to read the cards from her friends, the same messages written in each one; 'Congratulations, you're now legal... to ride a scooter', 'Congratulations you're now legal... to buy a lottery ticket.' Was sex some kind of joke to them?

Cara finished opening the presents and lay back on the grass, torn paper all around her. She held a palm flat against her forehead to shield her eyes from the sun as Chloe poured her another glass of champagne.

They looked so alike, Cara would introduce her as a big sister, another joke that wasn't really funny. Cara had always wanted a sister. And Chloe a child of her own. Chloe had always had a lot of boyfriends but said she was 'waiting for a man'.

Cara's laugh floated like birdsong on the breeze. What would life have been like without a child? I remember the day we got the diagnosis. It was the first thing Laura said when we left the hospital; 'I don't mind dying but I can't give a child a life like this'.

'Aunt Chloe, maybe you could be my bridesmaid one day?' Chloe didn't say anything, just folded her arms across her chest

Chloe leaned forward for the champagne bottle She had a deep tan from all the far away places she had been. Unlike a parent, she'd never had to worry about travelling during school holidays. So she could always get her flights on the cheap.

'Why don't you try on my ring,' Cara said. Prosecco splashed over the rim of the glass that Chloe was pouring. 'I bet it would fit you; Mum still wore it until quite recently.'

Chloe's grip on the wet flute tightened. She did not reach for the ring Cara held outstretched.

'What are you waiting for?' Cara said, laughing. 'Do I need to get down on one knee?'

Chloe's voice cracked a little as she said: 'Maybe we should ask your father'. I couldn't tell from the way she tilted her head whether she wanted me to say yes or no.

'I don't see why you shouldn't,' I said.

Chloe rubbed her hands on her thighs to dry off the Prosecco before holding out her hand to Cara. I watched the ring as it was forced onto her slender finger.

Chloe held her hand very still as she looked at the ring, I could see the reflection of the silver in her sunglasses, her lips parted a little, and I could see that her teeth were gritted. She took a deep breath in and tried to pull the ring off.

I pulled Laura's old tool box from the cupboard beneath the stairs; it left behind a clean rectangle in the dust on the shelf. I ran my fingers over the chipped blue paint, smelt the WD40. 'Every woman needs a good tool box,' Laura had said to me, years ago. God I missed the sound of her voice.

Cara was sat on the ground beside a tub of margarine and a bottle of washing up liquid. She was still crying. All the bubbles had gone to her head.

Her cry hadn't really changed from when she was a baby. I tried to catch Chloe's eyes to see if she was thinking the same. She looked at me but I couldn't tell what she was thinking through her big black sunglasses and I turned away.

Cara's friends looked awkward as they tried to comfort her. I bet they didn't feel so much like adults anymore. I looked over at Laura but her chair was turned towards the rose bed. She could have been sleeping for all I knew.

I took the diagonal cutters from the box with one hand, placing the other on Chloe's wrist. I felt the delicate muscles and bones tensing beneath her skin as I slid the bottom blade beneath the ring and squeezed the handles of the cutters. One cut. Two. The two halves of the ring shone briefly in the afternoon sun as they fell to the ground.

Then came Cara, crawling across the grass. I thought she wanted to pick up the pieces of the ring, but when she neared my feet she stood and hugged Chloe, wiping tears into her long red hair. Cara's t-shirt bunched up as they embraced and for a moment it looked like the shawl the midwife had wrapped her in. She would always be Chloe's whether she knew it or not.

I picked Laura up from her chair and carried her up the stairs. She was tired out from the day's excitement. I laid her on the bed; gripped her hands around the rolled-up cloths to stop her nails from digging into her palms.

'I wouldn't change a thing,' I said. She blinked six or seven times. It was unclear what that was supposed to mean.

I looked out the bedroom window; I could see Chloe making her goodbyes. 'I remember walking with her to the fertility clinic,' I said. "Any sister would do the same, it makes sense, it's the closest match you can get' you told me. 'You'll barely be able to tell".

I watched Chloe walking towards the house in her red Capris, her calves tensing as she crossed the lawn. Despite what I said, sometimes I do wish we'd done things differently.

Chloe was waiting for me in the hall by the coat-rack.

'Have you told her yet?' Her sunglasses were off and her eyes were narrow. I noticed the wrinkles around the corners and thought how she was starting to look old. She said: 'That was part of the agreement. You said you would tell her when she turned 16.'

She ran both her hands through her hair and then reached for her jacket. As she stretched her blouse rose up and I saw the C-section scar on her stomach.

'I'll tell her tonight,' I said. 'When her friends are gone. You're right, she needs to know'. I could hear Cara come through to the hall to say goodbye. I shrugged at Chloe and she shook her head at me, wearily.

They hugged on the doorstep. So much more than aunt and niece. I watched as Chloe squeezed her one last time before releasing her grip. I remembered being in the maternity ward and how cruel it felt to take Cara from her arms. As they parted I could see it hurt her no less to let go now than it had on that day.

Cara had recovered from the incident with the ring. I'd saved the two halves; promised her we could get it fixed, get it sized to fit. Laura was asleep upstairs.

It could wait. It could wait another day.

'How's Mum?' Cara asked as she closed the door. I put a hand to the wall to steady myself before I realised what she meant. 'She's happy,' I said. I hoped Laura was asleep and couldn't hear us.

'Me too,' Cara said. Her eyes were heavy from champagne and her cheeks glowed from where she had caught the sun.

'That's good,' I said. 'It's nice to see you that way.

She turned away from me, so I could stroke her back and neck, the way I got her to sleep when she was little. 'I love you dad.'

'I love you too,' I thought how our chat could wait for another day.

Family Language

by

Bridie Wilkinson

The first language that I learnt to speak was the one of my family. I uncovered an alphabet in the mannerisms of my father, practiced the sounds of my mother's laugh and structured my first sentences around my siblings. But I realised early on that their dialect was always going to be too loud for me, too obtrusive. No matter how far I pulled away from them, straining to find my own voice, they were always there. A constant echo in every word I spoke. I tried to tune them out, but the chords of my family were entwined around me. I relied on them more than I would ever admit. When my father told me that my mother had died, I realised just how strong those ties had been. Our perfectly formed melody collapsed into itself, and brought everything down to a tuneless, dull thud.

It began with a phone call. I was sitting in a car park, waiting for a space, when the phone rang. In the opera of my family, my dad is the bass. A steady, deep rhythm that controls the whole song, his tone perfected due to his career as a radio host. Danny Ray, the man with the velvet voice. Danny Ray, the father who I hadn't spoken to in four months. When I think of my dad, I never see an image of his face. Instead, I hear him. As always, the memory of his deep baritone rose in my ears, filling my car as soon as I saw who was calling. I leaned back, shut my eyes, rolled down the window, attempting to drown him out with the noises outside - but all I could hear was him, vibrating against the car windows and pressing into my skull. Irritated, I picked up the phone, only to hear nothing on the other end. 'Dad?' I pressed the phone closer to my ear, and heard his breath, sharp and ragged in the background. The roughness of it pricked at me and I sat up taller, now alert. 'Dad?' I said again, my voice barely audible in the silent car. I listened, and finally heard the reliable bass line of my father pull itself upward, choked out of his throat to deliver me three words. 'Leila...Mum's died'.

The sentence threw itself against me. I sat, motionless as it scraped and slid across my body, staring straight ahead into the car park, watching the drivers move carefully around each other whilst my father began to cry. I couldn't process it. It was too strange. The voice that I had grown up with, emitting from radios, silencing a dinner table, disciplining my siblings and me, was now completely unrecognisable. It was a sobbing, discorded whimper. I wasn't tuning into Radio Danny Ray Kiernan anymore. He was breaking, his voice faltering under the weight of what he was telling me, but I couldn't understand him, didn't know him. I wanted to hang up. Instead I sat in my car and let him cry until his throat was raw.

Sarah Laurent heard Danny Kiernan before she saw him. When my sister and I were obsessing over the ideas of true love and fairy tales, my mother kindly gifted us with a short, lyrical sentence that we would repeat over and over. 'Our mum heard our dad before she saw him', we would say smugly, products of a story that was straight from our book pages. The scene was so familiar to us that we could picture it instantly. Our mother: consciously tall, twenty-two years old, and well-versed in rough men in bars and false promises of drinks. Our father: dressed in confidence and a hand me down suit, his 60's fringe falling into his face. She orders a drink, and her elbow is nudged, spilling the drink down her new top. Just as she is about to turn to shout profanities, she hears him. His silky smooth voice wraps around her like a shawl and draws her towards the young man who is speaking, now apologising profusely in her direction. It was love at first sound. From that moment, she never stopped loving Danny Ray's voice, as devoted to it as his loyal listeners who carried his career from pirate radio to primetime. My dad became the beat that we all tried to follow, the tempo of our family defined by my mother's love for him. In the car, listening as Danny Ray lost himself down the phone to me, it began to sink in. We were all missing our metronome. Our rhythms would now always be out of sync.

I could feel myself edging away and blurring out of focus, when a sniff reminded me that I wasn't the only person in the car. 'Dad?' I heard his cheek brushing against the mouthpiece as he nodded in response. I opened my mouth to find the words to follow, but nothing came. I was lost in my voice. I cleared my throat, and tried again. 'Have you told Eve and Oliver?'

My father's silence spoke for him.

'Call them, OK?' He didn't reply. I was trying to imagine him, to find the person behind the voice. I needed him to give me a sign that would make what was happening feel real, but his lack of an answer was useless to me. The phone call was coming from the strange, uninhabited space that exists between caller and receiver, taut between the two of us and tearing with every second that my father's silence continued. I needed him to take control of a situation that I was in no way prepared to handle. For the first time in four months, I needed him.

I attempted one more time. 'Dad?' The word tumbled between us and I listened as it fell and disintegrated in the silence. My father cleared his throat uncomfortably and I wanted to cry.

'I'll speak to you later' I said.

The dial tone that followed let me know that he was gone. Danny Ray had left me with no words and no hope. I looked at the phone, suddenly detached from the conversation that had been holding me together. The line had been cut. I unravelled, dropping the phone to my lap as I buckled over. I pressed my forehead to the steering wheel, desperately trying to stabilise myself as my world shook around me. My chest felt like it was folding into itself, trapping my lungs in my ribcage. I was trying to wrench out some kind of sound but all I could find were strangled, rasping breaths that ripped themselves free and grasped at the air around me. There was no noise except from the sounds of the vehicles in the car park that I was in, so far away from where I should be. When I eventually started the car and drove home, I didn't speak. When the messages came from the siblings and the relatives, with time differences forgotten and condolences accepted, I watched, mute, as the sun slowly pulled itself away from the day. I informed my editors and friends of what had happened and I planned my plane journey home, all without saying a word. There were so many conversations to have, but there was nothing to say.

My mother hated the fact that I moved for work. Becoming a writer was my own form of teenage rebellion in a home that never stopped speaking. She never said it, but it was there, underneath her sighs at my slight accent, my refusal of family invites and my inability to keep up with the constant communication that she craved. Once, when she had sighed one too many times down the phone, I reminded her of how her mother was probably equally as disapproving of her life when she was my age. 'No, Leila' she sighed again. 'Your grandmother never sighed. She never made much noise at all'.

The Laurent childhood was one of silence. Empty, ominous halls in tall rented homes were my mother's playground. Grandpa Laurent was a foreign policy advisor, and he had no issue with uprooting my mother and his family, moving from country to country. With every new passport stamp, young Sarah hoped that this would be the home she needed. She would court the cities and towns that she found herself in, go on long walks with them and search, finding out as much as possible. My mother became guilty of being patriotic towards countries that were never truly hers; crafting an identity by stealing traits from the locals that she watched. European accents, American swagger, English manners. I used to sit in the kitchen and listen as she told me adventurous stories of her youth, marvelling at this otherworldly past that I could not attach to the woman who moved around me, half-distracted by the washing she had to finish or the dinner she had to cook. But whenever I would go too far in my romanticising, my mother's face would sharpen, her wistful tone would become monotonous and she would shake her head. 'No, Leila'.

Despite her best wishes, her children stole geography just as she had. In our North London bubble everybody that we knew was three-quarters this or two-thirds that. Bored with our simple English heritage, we adopted Sarah Kiernan's hijacked nationality. We all spoke with her faint, indescribable accent throughout our childhood, until puberty hit and it became too ridiculous for Oliver and me. My sister, however, decided to keep the illusion going. Her voice kept the wayfaring inflection of my mother's own accent, a subtle hint at something falsely foreign. I heard it when she called me that day, lack of sleep dragging her down a few octaves. I tried not to wince as she spoke to me and to not think of the likeness to our mother. Eventually Eve stopped talking. We both stayed on the phone, relieved at finding a comfortable quietness in each other's company. ¬

'Are you coming home?' she asked. In this, too, she echoed my mother. I had heard that phrase from her so many times, and had always sidestepped answering. Now

I couldn't avoid it. I opened my mouth, trying to think of a way to tell her that the home she was talking about didn't exist anymore. Because home for me was always with my mother. The house itself was inherently hers, her signature scrawled across its rooms with handpicked colour schemes and hand-me-down furniture. I couldn't imagine the house without her in it. Home was never about the place. It was about the welcome she would give us, the easy way that we all fitted back together around her, our voices perfectly harmonised against hers. No matter how far I had travelled and stretched the ties between us, I would return to her and it would feel like nothing had changed. I didn't know what it would be like without her there, and the unknowing terrified me. I had no idea what home was anymore.

The street below my apartment window had gone pitch black. The city had retreated back into itself, preparing for a morning that was only seconds away. Time was passing and I wasn't ready for the day to end. I looked at my watch. It was five to midnight. 'Leila?' I was balancing on the minutes that separated one day from the next, the minutes that separated the day that Sarah Kiernan had existed and the day that she had not. Eve didn't have that luxury. It was already tomorrow for my sister. I realised that her voice, no longer my mother's, was echoing mine. The same desperate need that my father had ignored was being presented to me down the phone, separated by six hours and the Atlantic.

'Are you coming home?' she asked again.

I brushed my cheek against the phone mouthpiece in response.

Frozen Out

by

Robert Sharp

'Maggie, can we talk?'

He says it as a question, but really it's a statement. His hands grab my shoulders and he manoeuvres me into the chair, his leather armchair. This manhandling reminds me a bit of when we would make love. William would grab me by the shoulders and position me on the bed, as if he was laying out his military kit.

I perch on the edge of the seat. The last time he sat me down for a chat it was to tell me that his prostate trouble was back, so now a tiny bubble of worry is forming in my stomach. I fold my hands together and place them firmly on my lap, holding my tummy in, keeping myself corked.

'What is it, Bill? I've got to put the sausages on in a bit.'

Now I'm sitting still he bounds over to the bureau and pulls out a white folder. It's some kind of prospectus. He grabs one of the footstools and places it beside me. He sits down, awkwardly. The stool is too short and suddenly he's all knees. I assume that he'll get up and find something else, but instead he hugs at his knees like a schoolboy.

He takes a deep breath, and begins.

'I've been thinking about my... arrangements. For when I... you know...'

'For when you die?'

'Yes.'

'Oh Bill! We went through all that last time, remember? I know John Hubbard's retired now, but Reverend Hale is a lovely woman, she'll do it well, and the hymns you picked are just perfect.'

He opens his mouth to speak, but I grab his wrist. 'Don't make me go through all that again, I don't like to think about it.'

I stand up. 'And anyway, there's nothing to say that its going to happen any time soon. It's just, well, the prostate, its just... back. There's lots we can still do. Don't give up.'

I make to leave for the sausages, but he puts out his arm like the policeman used to do at crossroads.

'Please, Maggie.' He proffers the folder. I sigh, and flop back into the leather.

'Be careful with the chair,' he says.

I ignore him. He is so precious about the bloody chair. 'What is it, Bill? What have you got there.'

His eyes tighten with enthusiasm as he opens the folder.

'This,' he says, 'is the prospectus for the Cryocor Foundation.'

I take the folder from him. It's made of thick card-stock and has a glossy, laminated cover. There's an illustration on the front: an abstract figure of a person in a box with lines coming out of them. Wires, maybe, or tentacles.

'Some kind of investment?' I ask.

He smirks. 'You could say that.' He waits for me to open the folder, but I leave it shut on my lap and just look at him. I can't really be bothered with William's schemes just now.

'The company is the world leader in cryonics.'

I shake my head. No idea.

'They freeze bodies in cryogenic tanks.'

I giggle.

'And and then...' He coughs. 'And then, they... erm... they wait for science to advance to the stage where...'

'... they can be resurrected?'

'Yep. Exactly.'

Oh, William! 'And you want to invest with these people?'

Now its William's turn to giggle. 'No Maggie. I want to be the one that gets frozen.'

There is nothing wrong with my ears. I heard him correctly. I stop laughing.

'You're joking.'

I look at him, still hunched on the stool. He stares back at me, scanning my face.

He's not joking.

I shake my head. 'Don't be ridiculous. It's... it's bonkers. It's a fantasy.' For the first time, I open the white folder and flip through the pages. 'Its a fraud!'

'No, Maggie, its not.'

'But they can't bring people back to life. That's ridiculous.'

William shakes his head. 'That's not what they do. They just freeze me. Then I have to wait for medical science to... catch up.'

The worry bubble inside me has burst, and now something hotter is growing in there. I put my fingers on my temples and massage my head.

William fills the silence. 'Basically, when you're on the way out, you call the standby team to come and freeze you. Then they take you off to Arizona where you're stored.' He pulls the folder from my lap, licks his fingers, and turns the pages. 'There's a picture of the facility on page seven, see?'

I don't look.

'You can have just your brain preserved if you want, but that seems a bit weird to me. So I'm going for the full body preservation option on page eighteen.'

I open my mouth and speak without thinking.

'And how much does it cost?' As if that matters.

73

It appears that William memorised the figures. 'Well there's the annual membership fee of seven-hundred-and-fifty dollars—that will probably rise with inflation, of course. And then the cost of the post-mortem treatment is three hundred thousand dollars.'

I bow my head. This is infuriating.

'That's dollars, Maggie. Not pounds.'

'Pounds, dollars, whatever. We don't have that money hanging around... unless you have some secret account you're not telling me about?' If there is one thing I know about William it is that he definitely does not have a secret bank account. The man can't keep a Valentine's Day present hidden properly, let alone an off-shore nest-egg.

And then he explains to me how we can release the equity in the house to pay for the procedure, but that I will be able to live here indefinitely, and it will only be sold when I no longer need it.

'Its not as if Becky and Roger need the money, do they?'

It is as if he has punched me in the chest. I look away from him, and to the photo of Becky on the coffee table. Our darling daughter on her wedding day, clutching the well-groomed, well-heeled, well-off Roger like a prize. No, they don't need the money.

Next to Becky's frame is another wedding photo, taken thirty-one years earlier. William and me, in the church porch, when we were both twenty-three. Two lifetimes ago, that photo. I remember the lace on the collar of my dress chafing at my neck, and clutching his hands so tightly as I promised to love, honour and obey. We still said 'obey' in those days, but I didn't mind. I wanted to be this adventurer's wife, and to be by his side as he travelled the world. He already had a vice-consul posting at the Embassy in Burma, and he said he wanted me with him.

So off we went, first to the church, and then to Rangoon. It was thrilling. Later we went to Nairobi, to Prague, to Paris, and finally, to Reigate.

I look again at the photo. It was a snap decision to marry William but I have never regretted it.

He speaks: 'Gerry and Ian think it's a good idea.'

Right. So he's discussed with his golfing buddies already, has he?

'I mean, Gerry's an actuary, right. He says that in cost-benefit terms it's actually a no-brainer. It might not work, but if it does then the payoff is infinite. And if I don't do it, well, then, I'm definitely dead forever.'

'We're all dead in the long run, Bill.'

'But maybe not! Don't you see? There are advances every day, Maggie. Didn't you hear about that Italian doctor doing head transplants and freezing monkeys? And that's right now, so there's sure to be something better in the future.'

He stands up and begins to pace. 'The only way to have any kind of chance to beat it –death I mean – is if I take steps to preserve myself for the future. Gerry says it's a bit like... what's that chap that Reverend Hale mentioned in her sermon? A Pascal's Wager. You know, where you might as well believe in Jesus, because that's the only way you'll get...'

'I know who Blaise Pascal is, Bill.'

He skips back over to the armchair and slaps me on the knee. 'Of course you do! Of course you do! Well then, you understand?'

'If Gerry thinks its such a good gamble then why isn't he doing it too?'

'Oh, well, you know, Carole wouldn't let him...'

I roll my eyes. He puts his hands on his hips and cocks his head as he looks at me. 'But you're not like that are you, Maggie?'

Comparing me to Carole is the last straw. I leap up out of the chair. He's startled, and steps back.

'I cannot believe how selfish you are being, William!'

He regains his poise, and shouts back: 'And I can't believe how short-sighted you're being! For once in your life, have a radical thought. I am reaching for immortality here, and I would like your bloody support!'

Now I'm angry and I need to be away from his face. I head for the kitchen and he doesn't follow. A moment later I hear heavy footsteps on the stairs.

I pull the frozen sausages out of the bag and slam them onto the oven tray. Why did I moan about the cost? Why did I call him selfish? I should have just come straight out with what I wanted to ask, but could not:

'Why don't you want me to come with you?'

Comfort Zone

by

Katie McCrory

Potential kidnap. Dengue fever. Poisonous spiders. Those were the things she was most concerned about until she read the polite notice in the information centre warning her about the leeches. That was a new one. She added it to her mental Rolodex of Things To Worry About, somewhere between the fire ants and the snakes, and pondered why – not for the first time – she had signed up to week-long jungle trek into the rainforest-clad foothills of Vietnam.

It was one of the Big Irritating Things he chalked up against her. That dextrous leap between contemplating life, and things that would almost certainly end it. Especially when he was out with the lads. What if they got into a fight and someone had a knife, she would ask, or if he stumbled in front of a car? It can be dangerous in South-east London, she reminded him. Every day.

The website had needlessly described getting to the start of the trek as 'part of the adventure' – something which generated a disproportionate amount of anxiety the night before as she lay on her hostel bed, swathed in a film of sweat, counting the ceiling fan rotations and willing sleep to take her away. The next day she spent five hours in a minibus having her coccyx slammed into potholes whilst the woman next to her silently vomited into a plastic bag.

Four weeks to the day before the trip, she bought a huge map of the world and opened it up on her living room floor. She had plenty of space, since he'd taken all the nice furniture. She stood in the middle, drinking in the ragged edges of the continents and the steadfast paths of the rivers tracking from mountains to seas. She felt like an alien that had veered off-course, trying to grasp the magnitude of planet Earth from the A205 South Circular and a two-bed semi in a cul-de-sac in Catford. As she lifted her right foot she uncovered South-east Asia. Vietnam, she said aloud, the word ricocheting off the empty walls. It's as dangerous a place as any.

She had decided to stay with a local family the night before the trek, rather than frequenting one of the more insalubrious looking guesthouses. A choice she immediately regretted as the toothless grandfather lashed her bags to the back of his motorbike and indicated she ride on his lap. The youngest daughter, a precocious 14-year-old with selective ability with the English language and sufficient character traits to mark her out as a psychopath, watched her unpack her rucksack in the sweltering heat like a predator.

She had casually mentioned Vietnam to her two friends once the deed had been done, her heart pounding with the reality of visas, vaccinations and the new hot-pink hiking shoes burning in her mind. Are you sure, Lisa? Isn't it a bit... you know, dangerous? Why don't we go for a girl's weekend somewhere lovely instead, get a facial and a manicure? That will help you get over him, Lisa. She had to excuse herself and sit on the toilet with her head between her knees to recover. She had already booked the bloody flights. There was no time for a spa weekend now.

She was appointed a guide and a jungle chef – two Vietnamese teenagers dressed like they'd flown in from East LA, all fitted viscose shirts with inane slogans on the back, baggy pants round their arses and those baseballs caps with the labels still stuck on. She assumed they would be changing out of their flip-flops once the trek got underway, only to watch one of them trade up his tattered plastic ones for a knock-off pleather Gucci pair and indicate they were ready to go. Perhaps they missed the visitor notice about the leeches, Lisa wondered, as she tucked her trousers into two pairs of socks and doused herself in Jungle Formula for the third time that morning.

We need to talk, he had said, standing at the bedroom door. It was a Monday morning. She was drying her hair, already late for work and conjuring up excuses to tell Nigel, her boss, that didn't include the words 'because I hate my job almost as much as I hate you'. She'd left her knickers on the bathroom floor again; he hated it when she did that. Just like he hated the cup on the floor, the coat on the bed, the orange peel on the sofa, the way she walked in those high heels she got on sale in Harvey Nichols that cut the circulation off to her little toe. I'll pick them up once he's finished, she told herself, as she turned the hairdryer off so she could hear him properly.

The teenagers didn't speak much English. Most of what they did was lifted from R & B music. After her enthusiastic bout of questions were met with blank faces, Lisa fell silent, their march peppered occasionally with recognisable words, as the guide – reminded of his job title – pointed out a few things worth noting. *Bird. Ox. Tree.* The jungle chef hung back half a mile behind them, making his presence known by swinging his machete into the occasional tree and howling along to the tinny rasp of some pop song on his mobile phone. Not quite the image the guidebook had brought to mind as it breathlessly described this 'remote and evocative' part of the world, Lisa thought.

He would be out by the end of the week, he had said. No need to get upset about it. It wasn't her, it was him. But, really, it was her, he had implied; she was imperfect, broken, faulty. She was holding him back, he said. She was scared of living. *Jesus, Lisa, do you want to stay in Catford all your life?*

When they arrived at the camp a full six hours later, the teenagers set about chopping wood, boiling water, and producing an array of blades from their bags. She had been keeping another mental list of things to remind herself to get worried about this evening, when she had the emotional wherewithal to contemplate the first night under canvas with two machete-wielding 17-years-olds, no mobile phone signal, no map, and absolutely no Vietnamese conversational skills. She added the new knife collection.

That night, she had lain in the middle of their bed just to know what it felt like. Habit eventually pushed her over to the right, curled into a foetal ball and making her body as small as possible. She had listened to the certain roar of the trucks making their way down the A205 and the foxes shagging outside. After years of anxiety about his safety, she had allowed herself the luxury of imagining him under the wheels of a car. It's dangerous in South-east London, she reminded herself.

This night, she lay wedged in her hammock suspended above the floor of the camp shelter as her feet throbbed. She listened to the uncertain hoots of the forest and the laughter of two teenagers mucking about on their phone. After years of damning the wall of fear, she allowed herself to let go, completely. Releasing it all into the thick black night, into her unknown future. She had not been kidnapped, contracted dengue fever or encountered any poisonous spiders. And maybe the polite visitor's notice had gotten it entirely wrong, because she hadn't seen any leeches either.

Lisa was living. And she had finally left Catford.

Last Orders

by

Paul Wiseall

'The thing is though, when I said corndogs he thought I said condoms, and it wasn't until I mentioned dipping them in mayo that the confused look on his face finally made me twig.' Jerry laughed when I said this, that classic too-wide grin of his filling up his face.

'Wow, you know you're ridiculous, right?' Jer took a too-big mouthful of his beer, the foam head spilling out the sides of his mouth like something from cheap porn.

'Yeah, *I'm* the ridiculous one, says the guy who wears ladies' clothes to Friday night beers.' I nod towards the grey hoodie he's wearing. It used to be mine but it always looked better on him.

'We both know it looks better on me,' he says and now it is my turn to laugh. I lean over and punch Jerry lightly on the arm and he fakes pain, clutching himself in faux shock. I catch his eye and right then his smile slips to a grimace and for a moment he's unreadable. I falter and it goes silent between us. There's an elephant in the room and I don't know how to tackle it.

'So,' he eventually says. 'Any other weird dating stories?'

'God, yes. I haven't even told you about the guy who argued that circumcision was just FGM for blokes and I--'

A noise rips through the room and the barman's hitting the bell and shouting, 'LAST ORDERS - bang bang - 15 MINUTES FOR LAST ORDERS.'

'Should we get some more?'

He glances at his watch. 'We've got ages. I'll grab them in a minute. Finish this story first. I'm expecting a car crash.'

'Well, to cut a long story short, it just got weirder and weirder. And get this, right, he wanted to open a hotel and it would only be for people who own sausage dogs.' I drain my lager and place the glass to the side.

'Okay,' Jerry says, holding his hands up. 'I give in. There's no way I can beat your dating stories.'

'Come on, surely you've been on a date recently that went wrong?' I smile expectantly, not knowing how I'll feel if he says he actually has been dating.

'Ha, no I may as well be dead for all the luck I'm having lately. It's a tough break when you are born with a face like this. No one wants you.' He points to his chin and I just want to kiss him. He's beautiful. 'There was one girl actually,' he says, and for a second, a flash of heat burns up my face and I think he sees it because he quickly continues. 'But that ended pretty abruptly a few months ago'. I let out my breath slowly and coo in sympathy.

It goes silent again for a moment and, unsure of what else to do, I flick the button on my phone. But no one's texted me. I glance around the room and I notice some people staring. They're all dressed up and staring at me through their carefully cultivated style – the women with painted faces and the men with comedy ties. They look like clowns, soulless and ridiculous and like they don't fit in my world. I look over my shoulder to see if they're looking at someone else but there's nothing but wall behind me. I give them a dirty look and turn back to glance at Jerry.

I want to tell him I miss him. I want to tell him that it's like I've been living under a storm cloud and all I want is the chance to tell him the truth. Yet, here I am, sat, glancing nervously at him through my eyelashes like I'm thirteen and back in French class passing love notes. To make things worse, I'm even sharing examples of my unsuccessful love life. What a catch I am. Tell me you love me, dammit! Tell me you forgive me!

'So, you didn't answer the question,' I say. 'What's the weirdest thing that's ever happened to you on a date?'

Jerry's brow furrows, he unzips my old hoodie and awkwardly pulls his arms out of it. Placing it on the chair next to him, he says, 'I don't know really. There's been some weird ones, but after your talk of hotdogs, one thing does spring to mind. It wasn't a date but there was a stalker.'

'Holy shit, you had a stalker? Does this make you famous?' I pretend to take photos with my hands.

'Well, I guess she wasn't really a stalker. I used to work with her. We kissed a few times and honestly, she was just insane.'

'I don't understand,' I say. 'Seriously?'

'Seriously! She was adamant that we were meant to be together. Get this, after she got sacked our IT guy found she'd forwarded a load of email dialogue we'd had in work back to her personal email.'

'That's just bizarre.' I lift my glass to my mouth to take another gulp of beer before remembering that it's already empty.

'No, I'll tell to you what's bizarre,' Jerry continued. 'We had a work party months after she left and she turns up, and no one has the heart to tell her to bugger off. And she kept trying to talk to me all night.'

'Poor girl, I bet she got all dressed up and everything.'

'But what did she expect? Did she really think I'd see her and we'd go home arm in arm? I mean, come on! And that's how I ended up inventing the sausage trick.'

'Are you saying you pulled your penis out?'

'No, you lunatic. This girl, what was her name... Kelli Samuels or something. God, I don't even remember. So, Kelli comes over and I freeze because I really don't want to talk to her, and without thinking I just grab a handful of cocktail sausages from the buffet and stuff them into my mouth. Then, before I've registered what I'm doing

I'm grabbing more sausages and some more and I just squeeze them into my cheeks and start awkwardly trying to chew this mouthful of cheap meat. I stare at her as if to say, 'Oops I can't talk as my mouth's full' and she... the expression on her face was unforgettable. I guess a gob full of meat will do that. And that's when I totally mess up and I laugh. I laugh so hard, meat flies from my mouth and hits her in the face. She flips her shit and starts crying. And that is how you end an awkward conversation.'

The noise cuts through the pub again and I hear 'LAST ORDERS!' - bang bang – 'LAST ORDERS!'

'Seriously, you better grab some more. Your round, right?' I nod to Jerry and then towards the bar where the barman's adjusting his hair piece. Jerry purses his lips and checks his watch. I don't want him to go. 'Come on,' I say, 'just one for the road.'

'Fine, fine, though I'm pretty sure I got the last round too.' He didn't and we both know this. I watch Jerry as he sidles out of the booth and heads towards the bar. I continue to watch him as he walks away and for a moment I'm overwhelmed with a memory. I push it away.

The clowns are still staring at me, and some of them have started to sneer. I pull out my phone to update my status but I can still feel their eyes on me. I shout over to them, what the hell are they looking at? But they don't respond.

Somewhere behind me the barman shouts again, 'LAST ORDERS' – bang bang – 'LAST ORDERS.' I turn back to my phone.

After what feels like too long, Jer comes back and places a drink in front of me. He hasn't got one for himself and I ask him why.

Jerry sits down and softly says, 'My time's up and I didn't realise.'

'I don't understand,' I tell him. I ask again, why? But he just sits there, smiling. I can't let him leave yet. I take a deep breath and for a brief moment I am back in my car, my foot to the floor and I'm aiming straight for that elephant in the room. That's when I say it.

'You look wrong,' it just bursts out of my mouth. 'This professor guy, he showed me pictures but I didn't imagine... I couldn't imagine.'

'Yeah, It's a bit different isn't it?' Jerry says with that smile still on his face. He rubs his fingers absently over the shredded skin.

'Does it hurt? I mean did it hurt, when it...?'

'Nah, it's like the hard skin on your feet. I could poke pins in my face now and nothing would hurt, look.' I wince as Jerry pushes a finger into the red flesh of his temple. The muscle is still all scarlet and raw as if it happened yesterday. His finger goes too far in and I flinch for him. Jerry notices I'm uncomfortable and removes his finger, wiping it clean on the hoodie. 'It's the friction apparently,' Jerry says. 'That's what some expert said. The friction caused my face to heat up, burnt out the nerves, cauterised them. Not that I remember, he reckons the impact probably knocked me out before I could register a thing.' Jerry smiled at this and for some reason I feel better.

'That's good,' I say. I don't have many other words. I want to tell him he looks like that Batman villain, Two-Face. The one who has got one side sexy and suave and the other side melted by acid. That's how Jerry's face looks. Melted with acid.

Jerry then leans across the table and with his clean hand he strokes my cheek. His fingers glisten as he pulls them back. I hadn't realised I had started to cry. I take his hand in mine and pull it back towards my face. His skin's so cold, like wax.

'I just need to know if you still love me.' I whisper it. 'I need to know if you forgive me but most of all, just tell me that it was me all along. It was me - it is me - that you love.'

Jerry smiles that smile. He leans across the table and I don't understand what's happening but while still cupping my cheek he kisses me. I close my eyes to savour the moment and when I open them again, he's gone. My whole world has gone.

I lift my pint back up to my lips and drain it. As I replace it on the table in front of me, something weird happens; the glass softens in my hands and becomes a white plastic cup. The room around me shifts, the dressed-up clowns are now seated in rows, still sneering at me is talking to me. They're mouthing words I don't understand. They're saying words like 'do you' and 'driving' and 'admit' and these words have lost all meaning so I just say, 'I don't understand.' They say 'Miss Samuels,' and I just repeat the same sentence, over and over.

From somewhere far away someone shouts above me and still I shout back to them that I don't understand. They're shouting 'Murderer'.

And that's when I hear something I do understand. The barman beside me shouts to the room, 'LAST ORDERS – bang bang – LAST ORDERS!'

The Merchant of Death

by

Tiffany Sherlock

I was so deeply engrossed in my writing, the words took a while to reach me.

But the voice was an unfamiliar one, authoritative and coldly clipped, and slowly it sunk in... *'I'm not dead.'*

A chill ran straight through my body, for it was a strange sentence, yes, and yet strangely familiar too.

Hunched over my typewriter by day, I rarely spoke to a soul. But I'd often heard that line in my nightmares. I'd once asked other obituary writers whether they suffered the same, and they'd all confessed to identical dreams, or variations thereof.

I looked up and saw my visitor.

He was bearded and smart in his crisp suit, and he gripped the wooden chair across from me, his face serious and his knuckles white. 'I'm not dead,' he repeated. 'It was my brother Ludvig who died. Not me.' His voice carried not just anger, but a deep and exhausted grief.

Even now, so many years later, that moment makes me squirm with shame. I recognised him, of course. I could have told you his life history with my eyes closed.

I'd written his obituary the day before.

The scion of a fabulously wealthy family empire, which sold arms and explosives, he'd personally invented dynamite. He'd revolutionised industry and modern warfare with his innovations. He was one of the most powerful men on the earth.

And despite the reports our newspaper had – wrongly – received the day before, and the obituary which I'd written, which was now gracing our pages across the whole country, Alfred Nobel very clearly wasn't dead.

And as he stared at me, I couldn't find a single word to speak.

I remained sitting in my chair, blinking in the dazzling light of his fame, his power, his very aliveness. My mind was so crowded with conflicting thoughts that

I could barely make sense of the moment. I wondered how he had managed to march into my little side office without my editor knowing. If he'd realised that the great – and the very alive – Nobel was in our building, he'd have been here within a heartbeat.

And I would have been flung out of the door just as fast.

Although, of course, my job was over anyway, as I would soon be a public mockery for declaring the death of the world's most famous man. 'My whole life is over,' I thought wildly. 'Nobel will make sure of that.' My career, my little apartment, my pride and reputation – all destroyed forever.

And all this time, as these wild thoughts swirled in my head, all he did was stare at me.

'I'm sorry,' I finally said. 'We received incorrect information.'

'Yes,' he nodded.

Having spoken I found I could break free of my paralysis. I indicated the chair before me.

'Please, take a seat?' I said.

Nobel did take the chair, but he sat stiffly and awkward as I frantically tried to think of words to calm the situation. But Nobel took that dilemma from me.

'The headline on my obituary, did you write that?' he said tightly. '*The Merchant Of Death Is Dead.*'

'Yes,' I nodded.

I momentarily recalled my pride at coining the phrase. It had been more dramatic and perhaps less respectful than our traditional obituary style would normally allow, but to my satisfaction it had made the cut.

But my words suddenly seemed cruel when I was faced with the man himself.

As the blood rushed to my cheeks, I felt like a shamed child and, just like a child, I wanted to cry out that it wasn't *fair*.

'You weren't supposed to read that!' I blurted out.

He was supposed to be dead. Not sitting and reading with horror my damning appraisal of his life's works. Nobel's stony silence was the most withering reply he could have given. Then he quoted another line.

'A man who became rich by finding ways to kill more people, faster than ever before.' Instantly, I knew that he would have been able to quote the entire obituary from memory. And then he unfroze and leant forward.

'What gives you the right to judge me?' he asked, his voice furious and low. 'I've achieved great things, changed the world.

'How dare you view me with such contempt? A small man in this little office, typing small words.'

For a moment I almost buckled under the weight of his anger, but one thing alone kept me standing straight. It broke through even my fear of my editor's rage, my looming unemployment. I was still a young man, an idealist, and now I couldn't keep quiet.

'I wrote it because it's true,' I said. 'It's *true.*'

I'd done my research. I knew he'd been a shy boy who'd loved poetry, before he'd been forced into the family business. Yet instead of rebelling against his fate, he'd flourished, developing an incredible talent for inventing explosives, fuses, blasting caps and mines. And those tools of destruction hadn't just blown up rocks and buildings. There had been thousands of men as well, flung up in fountains of blood and flesh across the battlefields of the Crimean and the world.

Fathers and friends, brothers and sons.

And it was that knowledge which gave me courage.

'Because of you, tens of thousands are dead,' I said and I felt my own anger rising. 'I couldn't ignore that. I'm paid to write the truth about people.'

'Miners, factory workers, their lives are *safer*. Because of me,' he fired back. 'You didn't consider that?'

As his voice rose to a shout, I remembered my editor in the main office outside. The truth was, I'd written Nobel's obituary on his orders. Of course, he'd have to fire me, to save face, yet there was still a chance I'd be compensated in private. But not if I angered such an important man now.

'I'm sorry,' I said again, holding out my palms in appeal. 'I never expected you to read those words. I meant no offence.'

'No offence!' Nobel said, standing up across the desk from me.

'Half the country has read what you've written by now. You've blackened my reputation. The world will think of me as a killer – because of you.' With that, rage fired up inside me, and it blinded me for a second to all sense.

'They won't think these things because of the words I wrote,' I retorted.

'They'll think it because of the things you've done.' As soon as the words left my mouth, I knew how profoundly disrespectful they were. I might not agree with Nobel but he was an incredibly talented and intelligent man.

And exceptionally powerful too.

He sank into his chair and took a deep breath, ran one hand over his beard. Then he looked me in the eyes, properly, for a long moment. There was no anger any more, just a searching curiosity.

'I want to know one thing,' he said. 'When you wrote those words, did you mean them? Or was it just for a good headline?'

The Merchant of Death.

Although unspoken, the phrase hung in the air between us, and I floundered, not knowing the best reply. As he waited for my response without a flicker of movement, I didn't see a monster. I glimpsed an old man, vulnerable for the first time. So I took a moment to really consider him, and his life's work. Was that truly how he was regarded by the world? Did everyone truly think that of him? Or was what I'd written merely the careless ego of a self-important young writer?

In the end, the question seemed too important for anything less than a truthful answer.

'I'm a pacifist,' I said quietly. 'I believe peace begets peace, and you have given the world a terrible new weapon of war.'

Nobel raised his hands and his eyes to the ceiling. 'I'm a pacifist too,' he said furiously. 'You young know nothing.'

Astonished, I stared at him open-mouthed.

'What I have created is the deterrent of war,' Nobel spelled out, as if to an idiot. 'When both sides know they can destroy each other completely, there will be *no war.*'

This was his belief? How could he be such a fool? 'War begets war, and weapons simply beget more weapons,' I fired back scornfully. I knew so little then, yet I was sure I knew it all.

He scoffed in response so I kept talking.

'You truly believe that the greater the weapon, the less likely there will be war? That a more powerful weapon can mean less death?' I clarified, half antagonistic but half curious too.

In response, Nobel sank back a little, and grew thoughtful. 'Yes,' he said finally. 'I do.'

Perhaps I was mistaken but there seemed to be a new emotion in his voice, separate from the fury he'd carried on his shoulders as he'd entered the room. Standing, he put on his hat and faced me, square-on.

'All those things you wrote, I'm sorry that's what you think of me,' he said.

I disagreed with everything that Nobel stood for. His strange idea that by helping to kill, he was drawing world peace closer, was a fool's delusion and a dangerous dream. Still, it was clear that he believed it, held strong by a strange integrity.

So I simply held out my hand. I found that I was praying for him to shake it – perhaps as a form of forgiveness.

Nobel shook his head, scornful at my cowardice. Then he turned and marched from the room. He didn't look back or bid me farewell, and I trembled as I sank back into my chair. Within the hour, I was packing my desk and being escorted from the building. It emerged that Nobel had sought my editor out before leaving.

I heard later that he'd been dignified in his complaint, but of course after such a public mistake, my editor had no choice than to fire me. I was briefly held up for derision across the land. But over time, I'd slowly rebuilt my reputation and my career.

And when Alfred Nobel did die eight years later, the news saddened me deeply. Perhaps my colleagues at my new newspaper asked me to write his obituary as a joke. Perhaps because they thought I was best qualified to do so. But I asked a colleague to write it, instead. In a strange way, I'd liked the man who'd confronted me so many years before. More than that, I'd never forgotten his pain at what I'd written. It had made me a better, more respectful writer – and man.

But of course, that wasn't Nobel's main legacy.

In his will, he left detailed instructions for the use of the vast wealth he'd amassed creating weapons and explosives. He instructed that it be used to create and adjudicate a series of international prizes, rewarding those who'd laboured towards world peace and humanity's greatest good. Nobel had never breathed a word of his plans to any of his friends, family or colleagues.

So no one could give any insight into why he had done it.

Of course, I was as surprised as anyone.

I'm too aware of the insignificance of my own life to claim any credit for his decision. But sometimes I recall the anguish in the eyes of the man who stood across that desk from me.

And I know that while my words have been long forgotten, his will live on forever.

> *Unmarried and childless, Nobel was a fabulously wealthy arms manufacturer, whose inventions included dynamite and detonating caps.*
>
> *His discoveries revolutionised mining - and warfare.*
>
> *He told no one of his plans to create the Nobel prizes.*
>
> *But eight years before his death, his brother Ludwig died, and a newspaper mistakenly published Nobel's obituary.*
>
> *It called him the Merchant of Death, grown rich from helping to kill men faster than ever before. All else remains speculation.*

Let's Play

by

Niall Alexander

We were just strangers on a train. That old refrain.

I'd seen him before, of course. You can't catch the same train at the same time from the same station to damn near the same destination five days a week for a period of years without encountering a few fellow unfortunates.

As he took the seat next to me, a slight smile on his face that said how sorry he was to have invaded my space, it occurred to me that I knew more about this man than I did many of my friends. I knew that he usually took the 17:35 as far as Falkirk Grahamston, the stop immediately before mine. I knew the store his clothes came from; I'd spied the bags. I knew he respected his elders; I'd watched him give up his chair on the same occasions I'd made myself small in mine.

Yet as familiar as I was with him, and he with me, I imagined, neither of us had said one word to the other. He had his spot at the back of the carriage and I had mine in the middle. He'd sit with his headphones on, happily tap-tap-tapping at his tablet, while I buried my nose in my phone, waging war on my inbox if I could be bothered.

But that day was different. The Fringe Festival was in full swing, so the 17:35 was packed when it spilled out of the city. Having waited an age at the security gates to be sure of securing my usual seat, I was leafing through the book Neal had begged me to buy for his birthday when my commuting counterpart settled beside me. He made no move to take his iPad out of his pixel-patterned messenger bag—the first warning that he fancied a chat.

Much as I knew about this man, I had never learned his name. He must have been thinking the same thing.

'Steve,' he said in a soft voice that fitted his easy features.

I nodded, noncommittal, suddenly afraid that his awareness matched mine. Afraid, especially, that he remembered the weeks I'd wasted blinking back tears over my boss's cruellest comments as acutely as I remembered the month he'd spent experimenting with that mistake of a moustache.

This was not a conversation I craved. Not today, anyway. A morning of important meetings had gone to shit after one of my colleagues had quit, and absent anyone better to blame, I'd borne the brunt of my perpetually harassed manager's anger. The last thing I needed now was a spot of awkward small talk with a man I'd rather remain a mystery, so I fixed my gaze on the page: an illustration explaining how to make something called a Creeper with just paper, patience and a pair of scissors.

But Steve soldiered on, indifferent to my ignorance. 'Is that this year's *Minecraft Annual*?'

Keen to bring this conversation to a conclusion as soon as humanly, I exhaled my frustration as I let him look at the book.

'One more thing we've got in common,' he noted, not at all rebuffed. 'Truth be told, though, you didn't strike me as the type.'

I sat up straighter and turned to face him. I'd had to grin and bear so much unfairness that day that I wasn't prepared to let another implied slight slide. 'And what type is that, exactly? You think I'm too girly to play video games? Is that seriously what you're saying?'

I regretted my outburst straightaway. Steve's smile had been wide; now, head hung, he looked as stricken as I'd felt earlier.

The train chose that second to sigh to a stop. A handful of passengers disembarked. Without them, the carriage was close to quiet, and I found myself missing the noise they'd made.

Before long, the outskirts of the city turned into towns; the towns gave way to fields of wheat and radiant rapeseed; the fields fell to fallow land and, as I watched the world beyond the window melt away, my heart softened with the scenery.

'Sorry about that, Steve,' I said into the silence.

'Me too,' he mumbled. 'Stupidest thing I've said all evening.'

'That may be, but the bad mood is on me. I've had... just the worst day at work.' Steve's expression seemed sympathetic. 'That's no excuse, though. I know we're not friends or anything, but please, let's not be enemies. Train acquaintances?'

'Train acquaintances,' he agreed with a small smile.

I didn't know then and I don't know now what compelled me to keep talking. I'd gotten exactly what I wanted; Steve was already searching through his satchel for less confrontational entertainment. But I felt worse instead of better.

'So when you said I didn't strike you as the type? You were right. This,' I indicated the Annual, 'is for my nephew. He's turning nine next month. Can't imagine why he wants this, though.'

Steve still looked like I'd stuck a pin in him, but to his credit, he recovered rapidly. 'I... I can think of a few reasons. One or two. I'm not sure about the book, but... hey,' he brightened slightly. 'Have you ever played?'

'Not exactly. But...'

'But?' He held out a hand, as if to catch my answer, and it dawned on me that I didn't want to disappoint him.

'Call me *Minecraft*-curious. I have tried. Like, a lot! But I just don't get it. Whereas Neal—that's my nephew—goes on and on about it. If he isn't swinging his pick—'

'His golden pick?'

'His diamond pick, I think.' Steve snorted his endorsement. Warmth washed over me as I went on, and it wasn't from the windows. 'If he isn't whaling on his world with that, he's watching those... what do you call them? Those videos that are all over YouTube?'

'Let's Plays, eh?' My travelling partner sat back. 'Huh. I wonder if he's watched any of mine,' he said.

'You make those? I thought you were... well, I honestly don't know what I thought.'

'Oh, I bet you could hazard a guess.' Steve shuffled in his seat. 'In all the ages we've taken this train, I know I've, ah... I've wondered—'

'—what I do?' He nodded, relieved that I'd read ahead rather than embarked on another rant. 'Me too. I mean, I've wondered what *you* do.'

His grin revealed a row of neat teeth. 'Ladies first,' he urged.

'That's how it is, is it? Then I guess I had you pegged as someone who works with computers.'

'Doesn't everyone? Don't you?' It was clear from his jovial tone that I hadn't offended him again.

'A man who insists on specifics! Alright. Point taken. So... an IT guy, I guess?'

'Close! But no—though I was, once. These days, I'm a design technician according to my job description, meaning I turn drawings into computer models for a small army of architects in the West End. But probably not for much longer.'

'How come?'

'Layoffs. Loads of layoffs.' His voice got so low that I had to lean in to hear him. 'I think the company's going under, and I'm what the spreadheads—sorry, the HR department—call non-essential personnel. It's only a matter of time before my neck's on the chopping block.'

I was lost for words. Even the thought of losing my job made me feel faint. Though it wasn't always wonderful, work was my world. But Steve didn't seem particularly bothered by the prospect.

The train stopped again. We were already halfway home, I noticed. How were we were already halfway home?

'Tell me, then,' I said as soon as the doors had closed. 'What do *I* do, detective?'

'Something with customers,' he answered immediately. 'Marketing, maybe? You've got a friendly face. A nice way with strangers—including eejits like me. And you're always on your Blackberry. Working all the way home?'

'Not today, but you're not wrong about the rest,' I responded. 'I'm in publishing, in publicity. I sort of sell stories.'

'And I bet you're brilliant at it,' he finished, so confident of his opinion that, I admit, it lifted my spirits.

'I certainly give it all I've got.'

'And no one can ask for more than that.'

Strange how it can take a complete stranger saying something for it to finally sink in. These were words I'd heard a hundred times from concerned friends and family members, but it was only then that they made sense. I'd given my employers everything, and if that wasn't enough, what in the world would be?

We shared a silence markedly more companionable than the last as I unpacked that. 'So you're not worried about losing your job?' I asked as we neared another station.

'Nah. It's not like I love it. And there are the Let's Plays, like you say. Believe it or not, they bring a bit in. Whenever someone like your nephew watches one of my streams, he—or she!—has to click through an advert or two. I've already got like, ten thousand subscribers, and the more the moneyer—'

'*Ten thousand?*' I was, perhaps, a little taken aback.

Steve had the good grace to look chastened. 'I'm not sure what they see in me either. I just make buildings out of blocks and talk. Anyway, either way, I'll be okay.'

I was about to ask him to help me understand my nephew's *Minecraft* mania when an automated voice announced that the next stop was Steve's.

'Hey,' he said as he stood. 'Maybe you and Neal might like to be in a Let's Play, one of these days.'

'That,' I started—

—and stopped, surprised by what I was set to say. He waited patiently while I thought through the consequences before forging on. 'Actually, that sounds like a better birthday gift than this daft *Annual*. He'd be over the moon, I'm sure. But someone will have to show me the ropes.'

Steve looked so stoked at the possibility of spending more time with me that I felt a telling tingle. 'I just so happen to have *Minecraft* on my tablet. How does tomorrow sound to you?' he asked as he shouldered his satchel. 'Same train, same station?'

'We can even sit at the back if you'd rather,' I replied.

Steve was beaming from ear to ear as he started towards the gap. And that might have been that. Except that he stopped. Turned around. Said: 'You never did tell me your name, train acquaintance.'

Thus the deal was sealed. He had made me laugh at the end of a truly hateful day. So I told him.

We didn't stay train acquaintances for long. By the time he lost his job we were fast friends, and I was starting to make sense of the game that had gotten us talking. We spent any number of nights online after that, collaborating on a cake the size of a castle for Neal's live birthday party. When that video brought in a bunch of new viewers, we started thinking about the next thing.

That story you probably know. He told it. I sold it. I got the word to a few specialist sites; they shared their pieces with the media; and a feelgood 'And Finally...' on the nine o' clock news mainstreamed our impending *Minecraft* marriage, so that almost a million people watched us tie the knot.

My nephew made for a resplendent ringbearer that day, but he wasn't invited to the virtual world Steve showed me a little later. It flummoxed me at first, just as my husband had. Neither of our characters had anything in our inventories, and I noticed none of the architectural marvels he had made his name creating.

'What is this?' I had to ask.

'Nothing to write home about now—a new level no one but you and I need to know about—but with a little work? Well, the world is what we make of it, and I was hoping we could make this world into something special together.'

And we did.

The House

by

Eleanor Pender

The kitchen had always been his favourite room in the house. The low ceiling with old oak beams. The whitewashed walls of beautiful, irregular old stone. The Aga, our mother's pride and joy, standing under a multi-coloured mosaic of an archway. He had been so proud of that archway, the masterpiece of his mosaic career, he'd said once. Or what others might call the result of two enthusiastic 10-year-olds and boxes of mismatched broken titles.

I always thought it was the table that made the room. Slap bang in the centre, a traditional wooden kitchen table. Sturdy as a rock and looking as if it could last ten lifetimes. We'd sit around it, the three of us with Dad whenever the old electricity generator tripped up, and we'd play dominos by candlelight. Dad and Sylvie were always the best at dominos. We'd play round after round adding up the score, and the two of them would end up fighting for first place. The score sheet would even come out at breakfast the next day so our mother could hear of Sylvie's victory.

Now, seeing it again all these years later, the afternoon sunlight playing across the room and picking out shards of blue, green and yellow, it's not the table I'm looking at. My eyes keep returning to the mosaic archway. Those magical colours witness to so much at the centre of everything, where the five of us would gather to eat and talk. There was one time when there were three generations in the house at once - I think it was Grandma's 80th birthday - some event important enough to get everyone together. The double doors were thrown open to the garden and we set the table up with as many leaves as it had, to make it as long as possible. Adults at one end, kids at the other. I can see my mother, worrying over the food but so happy to have everyone there, even with Grandma calling out orders from the head of the table.

The door to the pantry is open now. It's a barn-style swing door split into two pieces. As kids, we used to measure our height by how much we could see over the bottom half, or how much of us could be seen from the other side. I'd be in the pantry, my back to the door, my head as far back as it could go to make me as tall as possible, my ponytail bumping against the wood. Benny and Sylvie would judge from the kitchen. Sylvie had never been the best judge though, saying I was taller than I was while Benny would correct her. I suppose she thought she was telling me what I wanted to hear, camaraderie between females, while he would tell the truth even if he knew I wouldn't like it. He had a realistic, honest approach to things, my twin brother. My best friend. How things change.

If he was here now, he would be sitting on one of the chairs, leaning back with his right foot balanced on his left knee. Benny always sat like that, opposite the kitchen sideboard and the big window looking out into the garden. The window stretches across close to the entire side of the room.

Looking out of the window into the garden now, I feel a tingling wash down my back and the hairs on my neck stand on end. He is behind me. He is sitting there. I turn and look but his chair is empty. I could have sworn he was there, leaning back and craning his neck to admire his mosaic. Our mosaic. I walk back over towards the Aga and run my left hand over the mish-mash of pieces embedded in the wall. Tiny slivers of every colour imaginable, some as big as your palm.

I stop at a jagged turquoise piece. My favourite one. I trace the edges with my fingers as I used to. The last time I stood here and felt this broken bit of pottery had been that night, the night where Sylvie-- The memory of why I stayed away, why everyone stayed away, overwhelms me. I try to push it out, to ignore it but standing in the kitchen next to the table, under the arch, it's too much. The screaming and crying fills my head and tears begin to stream down my cheeks. I see myself as I was then, a gangly teenager with holes in her tights, holding onto the wall with one hand, Benny standing next to her gripping the other. Adults and police walking around, murmuring, making notes. People fill the room, but nothing is happening. No-one talking to us, no-one is telling us anything, until Benny can't take it anymore. He screams her name and crumbles to the floor, his body shaking with sobs. He still has hold of my hand and pulls me down with him. I can see us now, our younger selves collapsed in a heap under the archway, not understanding where Sylvie has gone and why there are so many people around and why no-one will tell us anything.

It wasn't until Benny screamed and I held him as he sobbed that deep down I knew Sylvie wasn't coming back.

I need air. I need to get out of the kitchen. I yank open the back door and run into the garden. The day is fading down the valley, everything is so quiet and yet my head is pounding.

Why have I come back?

Because they left you the house.

But *why*?

Because you were the only one left.

I am the only one left who cares.

Tears run down my face as the honest voice, Benny's voice, responding to my anguish, echoes in my head. Imagining what he would say when he is not there to say it himself. Is that better than not thinking about him at all? Benny would have made this day easier, but they couldn't find him. I couldn't find him. But then again, do I want him here after what he did? I glance back to the kitchen, the last time I was here and confronted with his letter. Leaving medical school. Going to look for her. He'd seen our parents just the week before and had said nothing. I'd thought he was strong, but does sending a letter make him a coward? Abandoning all of us on some fool's errand? She was gone and not coming back. I was the one left behind. And then he was gone too and never came back. A postcard here and there, but they soon dropped off. He had always been terrible at staying in touch. He must be good at hiding now if inheritance lawyers can't find him.

Benny made his choice, and he never let me make mine. Maybe he knew I didn't agree with him, that I'd have talked him out of it. He was all I had and he never said a word.

I close my eyes and breathe in the warm air, the smell of a late British summer's day. In and out, in and out. I hear a familiar rustling as a light breeze blows through the willow tree. I feel calmer. The noise in my head quietens, and when I open my eyes, I am alone.

I turn and look at the house. I haven't thought about this house in so long. It is intoxicating, how the memories overwhelm me. It feels like an extension of us, a physical embodiment of our family. I look at where I grew up with a brother and a sister, and I know why my parents moved and left it behind. Our parents, my parents. They couldn't live here anymore. Just as I couldn't visit here anymore. I never wondered what happened to it, it didn't cross my mind. It wasn't until after the funeral I learned they still owned it. Is it possible for a place to hold memories of what happened in the exact spot where they happened?

For them to remain where they are, and you can close the door and leave them behind? I hope so.

I've made my choice. I expect to feel relief but instead it is more like, resignation. I am tired. I wait. I wait for the guilt, for the sense of familial responsibility. It doesn't come.

I walk through the kitchen straight to the hallway. I see the estate agent standing there. She is looking up as she admires the staircase and thick oak beams criss-crossing the ceiling. Up. It's the first place people look when they enter this house. I always thought it was strange.

She turns as she hears my steps on the tiles. I nod and make a move towards the front door.

'You don't need to see it all?' She looks at me, her hands clasping her folder. I don't care if she can see that I've been crying.

'No, I remember it well.'

'And? What's the verdict? It's a beautiful property.'

I take one more look at the staircase. The fading sun has come out and I catch flickers of colour dancing on the wall in the kitchen.

I face her, 'You can sell it, but on one condition.'

The estate agent looks at me, almost eager at the idea, 'Yes?'

'My lawyer will act as trustee in my stead and I never come back here.'

I turn and walk through the front door and up the gravel driveway, away from the house and into the early evening.

Suspended Reality

by

Sam Holl

...And so I just lay there, holding her.

If I'm honest – right then – there wasn't a sight, sound, vision or memory that could shake me from that position. Tears were still damp on my cheeks, the words ringing back and forth between my ears, kicking me between the eyes each time they passed.

'I can't give you what you want,' she'd said.

Who the hell did she think she was? I'd known her for a month, and spent no more than eight days in her company. What qualified her to know what I wanted?

But she knew. Oh my god, she knew. She'd known from the minute we first talked, and she'd kept that knowledge safe inside her mind until we'd found ourselves there. Until that moment. That bed, that room.

It had all happened so fast. From flirtation on Fraser Island to walks on white sand in the Whitsundays. To tonight, crying in Christchurch. What a rubbish end to such a promising journey. It was like I'd set out to win the World Cup, and ended up losing to San Marino in the qualifiers.

Let me take you back.

I'd never anticipated meeting anyone on the trip; that was far from the plan. This was a once-in-a-lifetime, round-the-world, drink-all-you-can type holiday. It was seven months of best mates travelling together: George and me with dreams of new beers, new experiences and forever-kept memories.

We achieved all three of those objectives. By that point, we'd tried Singha, Chang, Toohey Blue, Toohey Black, Castlemaine (the proper stuff), VB, Steinlager, Crown, a whole host of them. We'd been propositioned by prostitutes, survived a jet-ski crash, met great people, narrowly avoided several fights, nursed a sick campervan along Australia's east coast, spent way too much money and never looked back.

The beer, and the experiences, ensured that the memories would be plentiful and long-lasting. Even before she came along.

Fraser Island was where I first met her. George and I had been joined for a few weeks by our friend Tim, who'd just split up with his girlfriend and had come to Australia to blow away the cobwebs. The Fraser trip was certainly a perfect recipe for that: take a 4x4 and a load of beer and food onto the world's largest sand island (a UNESCO heritage site, no less), and camp for two nights. If we could avoid being eaten by a dingo, we were going to have a lot of fun.

We were put into 'teams' of people at the hostel the night before, with ours comprising the three of us and seven other randoms. She was one of those.

In the nicest possible way, there was nothing special about her when we met. She was a loud-ish northern girl who was clearly hiding something more fragile underneath that confident veneer. Like me, I suppose.

But she smoked, and so did I back then. In fact, at the time, I found it an extremely attractive characteristic in members of the opposite sex. So that's how it started, with cigarettes at the hostel bar.

The next few days were some of the highlights of the whole trip. As a team, we drove around the island, took in its sights, swam in freshwater lakes and drank until dawn. All the while, she and I grew closer with steadily increasing levels of flirtation throughout the hot, hungover, hazy days.

When the stint on Fraser came to a close, we all returned to the hostel and, naturally, there was an excuse for yet another drinking session – to celebrate our safe return from the deadly dingoes.

It was that evening that we had our first 'serious' chat. I can't remember exactly who initiated it; potentially me in a more-than-inebriated state (which is never ideal). We ended up talking about our history with relationships.

Mine was a simple tale: one of a commitment-phobe who'd spent a few years purposefully avoiding any kind of meaningful connection with women. Hers was rather more complicated – she'd come to Australia to escape a failed engagement and to clear her head. This had all happened about six months previously, so she was over it and enjoying her newfound freedom.

We talked for hours. Every subject from favourite foods to favourite music and favourite cities was covered. It was good, it was extremely good.

The next day everyone went their separate ways – but, as is often the case with travelling (particularly along the east coast of Australia), people are generally headed in the same direction. This applied to us, and there would be an overlap within a few days at the Whitsunday Islands. A plan was made.

We traded a few emails in the days between Fraser and the Whitsundays. Mainly for functional reasons – which hostels we were both planning on staying in, where we'd meet, how we could ditch other travelling companions to get some time alone, that kind of thing. But the undertone to these electronic exchanges was one of two people with common goals: to see how far we could take this dalliance, and how real we could make it.

Things started to get very real indeed.

Between the Thursday and the Saturday, I fell for her in a big way. As with Fraser Island, I'm sure the surroundings in the Whitsundays helped – look up some internet pictures of Whitehaven Beach, where we watched the sun go down together, and you'll see what I mean.

But it was more than that – she seemed to get me. To understand that, despite the thrill of meeting someone I really liked, it scared the shit out of me to have done so. She said she understood, that it was the same for her in light of her recent break-up.

On the last day in Airlie Beach, for me especially, panic set in that it was coming to an end. Our paths were not set to cross again on our respective travelling journeys, and it was going to be two months before either of us returned home. So I put another plan to her.

'Come and meet me in Christchurch.'

She'd had no intention to go to New Zealand but, as I did and it was an easy flight from Australia, it seemed perfect place within which to continue what we'd begun.

She arrived in Christchurch three days ago.

I thought it was all going swimmingly. We'd been out for nice meals, gone to a comedy show, shared a fair few bottles of red and had a great time. I started to formulate even more plans for when we got back to the UK.

Where would we live? She was from Leeds, and I was from London. Well, I'd never felt any particular allegiance to being in the south of England so, sure, I'd head up north. No problem.

Aha, but what would I do for work? Easy! Leeds had a pretty vibrant PR and marketing scene – I'd find a job there.

And, my goodness, if we were going to get this serious – we'd need to meet each other's parents, surely? We'd have to sort out some meetings when we got back on home soil.

Naturally, I didn't mention any of these ambitions, but they were there for when I needed them. For when the time was right.

We never got that far.

On our last night together we went out, big-style. We met up with George and two Irish girls he'd befriended and begun travelling with. There were pints and shots and strawpedos aplenty. For the majority of the evening, everyone seemed to be wrapped up in the general merriment and there were smiles all round.

But something was amiss. Again, beneath that crowd-pleasing veneer, she didn't seem quite right. I tried to sound her out about it when we got back, but she shrugged it off, told me to stop being stupid. She had her last cigarette and went to sleep. I did the same and figured that, whatever it was, it could wait until the morning.

'We need to talk,' came the words. It was only 7am, I was hungover as hell, and she wanted to talk. Of course, I knew what was coming. 'We need to talk' - always the pre-cursor to a conversation you don't want to have.

'What is it?' I answered, trying to play it cool.

'I can't give you what you want.'

The words dangled in the air as I tried to conjure a witty reply. None came. I settled for this instead: 'What are you on about? What is it I want that you can't give me?'

'We can't be together. I'm not ready for it.'

'BUT I AM!' That's what I wanted to shout in her frustrating face. 'I've spent years avoiding relationships, running away, not bothering. Finally, I'm ready and you're ruining it all!'

Instead, the tears arrived. I've never really been much of a crier, but this was my time. All those plans, gone. All that emotional investment I'd made in her, for nothing. How could she? The tears arrived in abundance.

Between the deep breathing and other attempts to regain a modicum of masculine dignity, I asked her to explain herself. The break-up she'd been through before going to Australia was certainly the main one, but it's the words that she used to describe our situation that I'll always remember.

'We're not living in the real world right now. We're living in a sort of suspended reality.'

I wanted to argue with her. To tell her that: no, to me, this was completely real. That the ideas which had popped up in my mind over the preceding days and weeks were things we could actually achieve.

But, looking back, she was fantastically right.

She and I had met during a blisteringly hot and exciting Australian summer, and we'd spent our subsequent moments exploring the culinary and visual delights of antipodean islands and cities. About as far from British reality as you can get.

The conversation didn't last much longer. I watched her pack up her stuff and leave, without saying a word. I did the same, bound for George's hostel.

And that was that. I never saw her again.

Her – the first girl I ever let my guard down for. The one who took my heart in her hands, then scrunched it into a ball like a piece of used wrapping paper and tossed it away.

Steak While We Wait

by

Johanna Jowers

I'm in the armchair. It must be getting old. The cushions used to be all squashily supportive, now they feel uncomfortably saggy. I'm slumped against them, trying to find that sweet spot where I'm wedged in but can still reach the crisps.

If you ask me how I'm feeling, I say drained. In both senses. I feel empty on the inside, and simultaneously as if I'm stuck in an echoing tunnel of effluent.

What a day. I pinch my forehead a couple of times as if this will somehow disperse the fog of fatigue, then rub my eyes.

Big mistake.

They're burning, itching, unbearable – I remember too late that my fingers are coated in crisp dust. Sweet chilli flavour apparently, but there's nothing sweet about this pain. I grub in my pocket for a dirty tissue and wipe them ineffectually. Blinking furiously seems to work better. I reach blindly for another crisp, but the bag is empty. My fumbling fingers knock the bag to the floor. I swear. Honestly, what else could possibly happen to make this day worse?

I find I'm tapping my foot. I don't normally do that. My wife says I do, but she's always complaining about something.

There's a rustling and a cracking sound. Oh fantastic. My foot's crunched the packet. So now I've got dirty fingers and I've crushed the last of the crisps. I stomp my shoe down hard on the packet and ignore the crumbs on the floor.

At least my eyes have stopped watering. I pull out my phone and open the app with the sweets. It's true, sugar in whatever form is addictive. I play and play. I can never get past this level.

The back door swings open. 'Hello!' calls Claire.

I give a squawk of frustration. 'You made me mess up my level.'

I hit replay. Out of the corner of my eye, I see her put down her shopping bag and switch on the kettle.

'Tea?' she shouts.

I can't believe it. 'Why can't you bloody listen? You've made me lose the level again. I've told you not to interrupt me. You seem to think what I'm doing's not important. It is, ok?'

'Sorry.' She's clanking away out there, making herself a cup. She walks past me on the way to the sofa, dropping a kiss on my head. 'I thought you were just playing a game on your phone.'

'How dare you? You show me absolutely no respect! You don't seem to understand at all. I'm exhausted. I need to relax. If I want to play my game, it's important, more important than anything you could possibly want to say to me.'

'Yes,' she says with patronising calmness, sipping her tea. 'You've said all this before.'

'And you never listen.'

'I do listen. You need time to relax, I get that.'

'Well you never let me, do you?'

'Calm down.' A look of something like guilt passes across Claire's face.

How dare she say that? 'You don't tell me to calm down,' I say, trying to keep the shaking anger down in my voice. 'I was perfectly calm until you came in and wound me up.'

'I'm sorry.' Her tone is unacceptably light. She's clearly not sorry at all.

'Well sorry doesn't make it not have happened, does it? Where were you, anyway?'

She glances past me for a moment. 'I had to go out.'

I snort and go back to my game. If she can't be bothered to explain herself, I'm not going to bother either.

She returns to the kitchen to unpack her shopping bag. I can hear shop-dirty plastic packaging touching the work surface. I may have been home a little early today, but, honestly, there's no excuse for having left the shopping until the evening, it's just poor time-management.

'John?' she calls.

'What?' I shout.

She comes through, twisting her fingers a bit. 'It's just that-- '

Unbelievable! 'What? Why did you interrupt me again?'

She turns away, and I hear her mutter. 'Nothing.'

This is utterly ridiculous. I can practically feel my blood pressure rising. 'Nothing? You waste my time like I've got loads of it.'

'What do you mean?' She's suddenly defensive. 'Are you ok?'

She's doing this deliberately, she must be. I leap to my feet. 'Which part of shut up and leave me alone is so hard for you to understand?'

She starts to prepare dinner. I can hear her, clattering pans, chopping. She's put the radio on and she's talking back to the news. She can never just let me listen to it, she always has to talk over it, as if her filtering of the news is going to be better than me hearing it for myself and forming my own view.

The hiss and steam from what I'm assuming must be steak sets the smoke alarm off. I get up from the irrationally lassitudinous armchair and storm through into the kitchen where she is flapping ineffectually at the bleeping nuisance with a tea towel. I open the back door and switch the cooker hood to full blast. She. NEVER. Listens.

She's served up one of the steaks with vegetables and is about to plate up the second one.

Steak's my favourite. Not a good sign.

'I'm not hungry.' To be honest I'm feeling sick. I take myself back to my chair and my game.

'Fine.' She pours a glass of wine and takes her dinner to the table. She sits down, and begins to eat in silence. The unhurried scrape of the knife and fork intrudes more than her speech. When I can stand it no more, I get up and go through.

She takes a sip of merlot. 'Yours is in the fridge.'

'You know,' I say, 'if you'd asked nicely I'd have sat and eaten it with you.'

She gives what appears to be a bark of laughter, although I see absolutely nothing funny about what I've said. 'Do you want me to reheat it for you?'

'I can do it myself. I don't want it overcooked.'

I remove the Tupperware from the fridge. I put the vegetables into the microwave and turn to the steak. My stomach growls as I open the lid. The steak is clearly well rested. A flash fry and a decent lot of seasoning will make this just about perfect. I drop the steak into the still-hot frying pan.

Suddenly she's there at my elbow again. 'Sweetheart, there's a-- '

I give her a look. Its meaning should be absolutely clear, but she's opening her mouth to carry on.

'Don't talk to me now. Can't you see I'm busy?' I turn the steak over with a satisfying sizzle.

'But, darling-- '

'I don't want my steak to go wrong, can't you see that? I don't know what's wrong with you this evening. Are you being deliberately annoying?'

She withdraws to the sitting room and switches on the news.

I turn off the radio that she has left on. I make up a tray, then take my food through to the sitting room and settle again in my chair. Hmm. The addition of butter and a bit more salt has made what I'm sure would otherwise have been a fairly bland and tasteless meal palatable.

As soon as I place my knife and fork together on the plate, she's at it again, staring hard at me across the room. She might be grinding her teeth. I can't think why she indulges in such an unpleasant activity. She only seems to do it when I'm a bit tired.

She swallows. 'Darling, there's a voicemail,' she says in such a rush that I nearly can't decipher the words. 'For you,' she adds.

I look away from her.

I still haven't finished that game level, so I pick up my phone. She's said before that she hates my phone. She's threatened to throw it out of the window. She hasn't done it yet and makes no move to do so now.

'Darling,' she says again. 'Your dad rang.'

I say nothing. Somehow my silence is not making it easy for her.

'Can you please concentrate on me, just for a second, John, please?'

I lower the phone. She's linked her fingers and twisted her hand so that she can rub her thumb up and down against the rings she wears. It looks weird.

'Your mum,' she says.

My forehead throbs. I feel like the vein in my temple is bulging.

'She's in hospital,' she says. 'Again.'

I can feel my heart beating in my ears.

'He said not to come,' she says. 'Not to worry. He'll let us know if-- '

Why is she still talking?

'Oh, sweetie, I'm sorry. Of course we can go if you want to. He says she won't really know if you're there or not.'

She walks across the room and launches herself at me, leaning over me for an awkward hug. I don't put my arms around her. She had to say it, didn't she? If she didn't say it, it didn't have to be real, but now it is.

'I just need to be left alone.'

'OK.' She backs off.

'Dad called my mobile anyway.'

'OK.'

'He said he'd left a message here. You didn't tell me straight away did you? It was important and you didn't. You just went out.' I know that's not fair, even as I say it. But if she had been more organised and gone shopping earlier, then she would have been here when I got back.

She put her hand on her hip. 'You don't exactly make it easy to talk to you.'

'I don't make it easy? What about you? You bustle about, you get things wrong, you don't even bother to pass on messages--' My eyes are getting moist. My throat feels thick. The words are sticking. It must be the smoke from the steak. 'When you know I need to know,' I finish, hoarsely.

There's this nagging feeling in my mind. She loves me. But what good is that to me, what good is anything, if she can't make it all ok? No one can make my mum better.

She sighs. 'I know you need someone to blame, John. I know you are feeling angry and stressed. But darling, I want you to listen now. This is horrible, this whole situation.'

She takes a couple of steps towards me and strokes my hair. It's sort of comforting, so I don't brush her hand away. 'Sweetheart,' she says, 'I know you find it hard that she's ill. Your mum. It's not fair, it's awful and she's not going to magically get better, we know that. It feels like the end of the world.'

She pauses.

She's wrong. It is not just a feeling. For my mum, it really is the end of the world. The words arrive in my mind, but they don't come out of my mouth. Saying it would make it real. I look at Claire. Doesn't she realise, if my mum can die, so can I?

'I'm here, ok, I'm here for you.' She starts to stroke my hair again.

'If I could just get some rest, I'd be fine,' I say. I shift in my armchair.

'How's your back?'

I grunt.

'Maybe you can see the doctor about it. I'm not nagging. I can come too. Or not. Your choice.' I notice how hesitant she sounds.

I nod. Maybe it would help to get my back sorted.

It won't make everything better, but it can't make it worse.

Steak while we wait. I guess that didn't hurt either.

I pull myself up, and we hug like teddy bears.

On the house phone handset, a red light blinks. Two messages.

Another message.

It's probably just someone selling something.

It can wait.

Farewell Feidhlim

by

Lee-Anne Smith

Dublin 22 August 1857

My darling boy, I have only a short time to remember everything about you. Little Feidhlim, how new you are to this world! How bonny and fresh! I hope you are satisfied with the name I have chosen for you. They will change it, I know. To John or James or perhaps, Samuel or Robert. It matters not, but I want you to have a proper Irish name for this time that we are together. Clever Nora says 'Feidhlim,' given as a gift from me to you, means 'lucky'. Nora writes these words for me, for I do not know how. I have never been to school; I know not how to read or write. But I do have a voice and I tell her what is in my heart.

Dublin 23 August 1857

I am Eliza, your Mammy. Mammy? I cannot believe it is true. For I am just a girl. A washerwoman. Like you, I was born here in Dublin. I drew breath for the first time 18 years ago, a few minutes after my sweet sister, Ellis. My own Mam, Mary-Gladys, gave birth to all nine of us near the Liffey River, which she used to think was lucky. But now, I have shamed her. I have shamed the family. She does not want to know me. She won't know you, my son. God forgive her, she is so weary of everything in this life. T'was an Gorta Mor that finished her. Ellis and I were wee girls during the Great Hunger. And hungry we have been ever since. We will be forever hungry. Feidhlim, my wish for you is that you will always have enough and that you will share what you have with others. Always be kind, my bonny boy.

Dublin 24 August 1857

Feidhlim, my dearest. Today I studied your face, the shape of your eyes and nose and the curve of your mouth. I opened your perfect littIe hands that hold my forefinger so tightly. I sketched your dear face as you slept and when you woke. I can draw, Feidhlim, and very well too! My good mistress gave me paper for Reading the Cup for her; she always asks me to tell her what the tea leaves say! And I crept into the Carpenters'shop and took an excellent pencil lying on the bench. Thank you God, Mary and Jesus, that I taught myself to draw. Otherwise, how would I remember you? I would be desperate, desperate to see your face!

Dublin 25 August 1857
Bright little boyeen, if you ever read this, I want you to know that I love you with all of my heart. When you are a man perhaps you will understand that what I am doing, is for you to live the perfect life. I cannot take you into the workhouse; I cannot let you start life in a place for the worst of people. For sick and old. For idiots. For lunatics. I know you would not survive. You, fair child, deserve the best this world can give. Your Mam cannot fail you. Oh Feidhlim, Feidhlim you are looking at me as I weep for what I am about to do. Forgive me! Oh, I beg your forgiveness! And know also, that your Mam cannot be imprisoned there. For I won't be wasted in a workhouse. I have to be free!

Dublin 26 August 1857
My boy, even though my own Mam says I am the bad twin, I hope you will not think me wicked. Last night after Clever Nora wrote my words to you, I went to see my mistress. I have been so happy to be her ladies' maid. But now she cannot let me stay; I have to be dismissed because I have you. There is nothing mistress can do. A good washerwoman, I am. And even better at carrying her messages and combing her hair. Feidhlim, when I see she is unhappy, I sing and dance until she laughs

and claps her hands. I was so sad to see how mistress cried when she let me go. She said she will miss me, her faithful servant, but she won't see me go into the workhouse. There is a plan for us, Feidhlim. Don't worry, I know we will be all right.

Dublin 27 August 1857
In three days, boyeen, I will feed you, dress you and kiss your bonny curls. I will carefully pin on your chest your name, date and place of birth written beautifully by Clever Nora. I will carry you, ever so gently, to the place they call the Foundling Home, push your basket into the space in the wall and ring the bell. Nothing in this world will never be the same for me again; my heart will break. But, I know this is your best chance - you will be looked after. Mistress says you will go to a family in the country who will love and nurture you. Oh my Feidhlim, you will play and run barefoot in the meadows! I wish you health, happiness and freedom, my son. Mistress gave me two of the lavender ruffles I used to launder for her... I will put one on your tiny wrist and the other one I will keep for myself.

Dublin 28 August 1857
Darling wee boy, let me tell you more. I am terribly excited and scared all at once. Mistress has arranged for me to board a sailing ship to Africa with many other young Irish lassies and some families. I don't know if we will ever get to British Kaffraria or what will become of us in that wild place. That is why I cannot risk taking you. My dear mistress gave me a reference; she said I was 'respectable' - otherwise I couldn't go. Feidhlim, I have to go. I want to grow all the food I could only imagine in Ireland. But what will become of me there? Oh Feidhlim, God protect us!

Dublin 29 August 1857
Dear One, before we part forever, I must let you know of your father. He is the cousin of my master. He was a regular visitor to the Big House. Boyeen, he is a married man with a family of his own, so he cannot know you. I cannot tell you more, for I know not more. But as small and fair as your Mammy is, so he is tall and dark. Mistress feels so badly about what happened under her roof, but it is not her fault. I have finished your portrait; I will keep it with me. Always. I was afraid it would fade in pencil and I would never again see your bonny face, but Mistress allowed me sit at her desk and finish it using ink from her inkwell. Thank you mistress!

Dublin 30 August 1857
Today, Feidhlim, I am imagining what you will be like when you are a grown man. It is a torture for me to think I will not see you again, my boy. My only hope is that you will live a happy life. I have to let you go. Today I went to Our Lady of Victories to pray for you. I have begged the Queen of Heaven to keep you safe always. I have my small kit of supplies ready. Mistress always allowed me to keep the used tea leaves which I dried and sold. Today she gave me a small tea caddy as a parting gift. I have put your picture, the Carpenters' pencil and the lavender ruffle into it, ready for the voyage.

Dublin 31 August 1857
Today we say farewell, my little Feidhlim. I brought you into this world; but today my gift to you is a better life. You go your way, I go mine... but our souls will forever be entwined. The Lady Kennaway leaves Plymouth harbour soon. If I ever get to the eastern Cape I will become a tea merchant and spend my time drawing pictures of Africa's wild flowers. Mistress thinks I will be alright. Goodbye

Ireland, goodbye Dublin, goodbye everything I know. And goodbye Feidhlim, love of my life. I carry you in my heart.

Four Words

by

Kim Curran

Dad came to visit today. I heard the forced happiness in his booming voice as he flirted with the nurses, heard the anxiety in the shuffling of his shiny, brown (always shiny, always brown) shoes on the bleach-clean floor outside my door. And I knew, somehow, that when he left, a little more of me would be missing.

I haven't seen him in a few months. He says he's been too busy with work, but I know it's because he hates coming to see me here. I hate it too. Not because I don't like seeing him – exactly the opposite, in fact. He scoops me up in a huge hug and calls me 'Chicken' and I feel like I'm a little girl again and I don't want the hug to end. Not ever. No, I hate when he visits because it hurts so much when he leaves.

After he'd gone through his usual jokes about me being careful not to walk over grates in case I fall through the gaps he sat me down on the squeaky, tiny bed and took my two hands in his one huge one.

'We need to talk.'

When has anything good started with those four words? When has the world not become a little more tarnished, a little more broken, after those four words?

Dad knew it too. I could tell he knew that whatever he was about to say was going to crush me just a little more because he wouldn't look at me. He kept staring at the picture I drew when I was little: the one of the house with the purple sky and the mummy and daddy and little girl standing outside. I wanted to shrink, shrink down and climb into that picture – into that happy family. Hide in that red-brick house and wait for the rain to come and the sky to clear. But it was useless. The one thing I've learnt in this place: there's nowhere to hide.

'I have met someone.'

Four more words falling like stones on glass.

He went on and on about her and how happy she makes him and how much I would like her. About how mum and he had been miserable for a very long time and how it would be better for everyone if they moved on with their lives. But I couldn't take in what he was saying because my ears were buzzing and I couldn't breathe. It felt like all the air inside me was being sucked out.

Did you know that if you took out all of the space between the atoms that make up the entire human race, it would fit into something the size of a sugar cube? I learnt that in Physics. That's how I felt. Like all those spaces had collapsed in on themselves, leaving nothing of me behind apart from a crumpled up ball of stuff that no one wanted.

He was saying that I could come and live with them and that I shouldn't be in this place anymore. That it wasn't any good for me. He started blaming mum for me being in here, blaming her for putting too much pressure on me. I couldn't listen any more. I was moments away from imploding and blinking out into nothingness. I slipped my hands out from his and excused myself, went into the bathroom, and was sick.

There wasn't much in my stomach. The thing that lives there, its black tendrils crawling through my blood and into my brain, has been sleeping lately. But the cistern felt cool against my forehead and I felt the world come back into focus. Tarnished. Broken. But in focus.

When I got back to my room, Dad was staring out the window. It was raining so hard all you could see were the rivulets of water falling like a bead curtain. The branches from the tree outside scratched on the window like a witch trying to claw her way in. I didn't want my dad to leave. I wanted him to stay here and protect me against the witch at the window and the monsters under my bed, like he did when I was little.

He hooked his finger under my chin and tilted my head up to look at him. 'You're a big girl now, Chicken.'

My eyes burned from fighting back the tears and the thing in my stomach uncoiled itself, yawning. It will want feeding now. I didn't want to be a big girl, not if that meant having to feel pain like this. Not if it meant having to be alone.

But I nodded, and forced on my most practiced, 'I'm OK smile', the one that stretches my skin so hard it feels like it might tear. I didn't want him to see how much what he was saying was killing me because I've already hurt him so much. Because this is all my fault. I got ill and that's what started the arguments; dad blaming mum, mum blaming dad. Both secretly blaming me.

I always believed that they would be OK. That when I got better they would get better, too. But as he walked out of the door and the wind howled outside, I knew it was too late. There was no point any more. The one thing holding me together, the one thing stopping me from turning to dust and blowing away, had been the hope that I would go home and we could be a family again. Happy and whole. But now it's broken.

Broken by those four words.

Those words are like a virus. The only way to get rid of it is pass them on.

I force my shaking limbs to walk down the stairs to Dr Kaiko's office. I force my skeletal fist to ball and tap against the door. It takes all of my strength.

I'm invited in.

'We need to talk.'

In My Head

by

Daisy Buchanan

'I've been thinking, and I reckon it's time we had a little chat.'

'Bloody hell. What is it now?'

'Well, I'm just a bit sick of our relationship, is all. I'm fed up of the way you criticise all my decisions, actions and plans.'

' 'Just'? That is such a passive aggressive word. Can't you own all your ideas? Mean what you say?'

'That is exactly what I mean.'

'There is a reason I'm hypercritical. I want what's best for you. If I don't stop pushing you, what will happen? You need me. Every success you've had has been down to me. I look for areas of improvement. I won't let you rest. You went to the gym, what, four times this week? If it was down to you, you would have just sat on the sofa in your horrible, sweaty tracksuit bottoms with your hand down a box of granola. Mind you, four days out of seven is only just acceptable. What were you doing on the other three days, you lazy...'

'I had a lot on!'

'You need to make time.'

'I've been wondering about where all this comes from. I know your intentions are good, they're just unrealistic. I'm not Superwoman. I know I'm capable of a lot, and I'm delighted that you recognise my potential, but you can't just push me until I fall over.'

'Now you just sound bigheaded.'

'Shhhh! Hear me out. It's thanks to you that I have never got complacent. I've always had this voice spurring me on, helping me to search for the next thing, the bigger thing. I'm endlessly reworking, finessing, improving upon what I've got to offer. In moderation this is brilliant. But it's also stopping me from enjoying my life.'

"Enjoying your life'? What are you, a Roman emperor? You'd like that, wouldn't you, sitting on your arse eating chocolate-covered grapes all day long.'

'You are a massive fun-sponge. For one thing, you never give me a chance to catch my breath. I can't have an hour to feel proud of my work because you're always nagging at me.'

'You manage to have plenty of fun without me when you go off and drink all that wine.'

'What we need to do is sit down together and work out a compromise between what you want for me, and what you think I want for me. We do want the same things. I just don't want to get burned out. Slow and steady wins the race, after all.'

'I'm sorry I'm so negative. I do know I'm doing it. I've just never really worked out any other way to be.'

'That's OK. It's how you were raised. We get 90 per cent in an exam, and instead of hearing 'well done!' we get 'What happened to the other 10?' We've never, really, been allowed to just do our best, we just have to be the best.'

'It's so hard. Because somewhere, there is always someone better. Someone cleverer, prettier, thinner, funnier. I'm ashamed of you, sometimes, because you'll never be the best at anything. This is why I think you're a failure. That you'll never amount to anything.'

'Now, I could burst into tears and stop talking to you at this point, but I'm going to take a deep breath and explain why that makes no sense. Firstly, this ranking system you have is very subjective. Secondly, it doesn't really exist.'

'Oh? Go on.'

'Am I a tennis player?'

'No. You're crap at all sports.'

'Thank you. You want me to be the Serena Williams of all things - the world number one. Serena professionally plays a game that has a clear points system, and a definite way of working out who is the best at it. Serena has been playing tennis for pretty much all her life, and has worked with the best coaches and trainers there are. Obviously she has enormous flair, talent and ability...'

'I really don't see what this...'

'Shut up. What I'm getting at is - nothing we do can be ranked, weighed and measured in the same way. We have access to different resources. And yet you seem to want me to be the Serena Williams of everything, whereas even the woman herself can only be the Serena Williams of tennis.'

'So you think I should just focus on one thing that you have to be the best at?'

'No. We're all built differently, and I've decided that I'd rather be quite good at a few things than a world number one at one thing, and have no life.'

'Suit yourself. Idiot.'

'Think about it. When are we at our happiest and most high functioning? When we're working together, in harmony, on the same project. We both love to cook. If we make food together, you shut up for a bit, and stop criticising me constantly. We're not at odds, because we're not trying to be the best.'

'And now I think about it, I'm still a bit...mean. I always worry that you're going to burn things, or that you're not experienced enough, or you'll drop a pan on your foot. You almost never do.'

'Thanks. I mess up sometimes, though.'

'That muscovado tart? It was an experiment. You took a risk, it didn't work out, but it's good that you tried. You didn't do anything wrong. Also, I am very proud of you for not eating the whole tin of condensed milk. I know you wanted to.'

'Yes! That's what I need to hear!'

'You still made loads of other stuff, and everyone who ate it liked it. But the best thing was how calm you were, and resourceful. The vibe was good.'

'That's what I want. We've been trying it your way for years, and getting good but not great, great but not perfect - and steadily more anxious and miserable.'

'You'd rather be flawed - but happy?'

'Yes! That's my choice! And ultimately it is my choice, isn't it? I know that I handed you the controls a while ago - but I need to take responsibility. Tell you what I need.'

'It's going to take some getting used to, but I'll try.'

'And I'll stop trying quite so hard. Thanks, Brain.'

Actually

by

Amy McLellan

Years later, of course, the whole conversation, this pivotal turning point in their lives, was distilled down to just six words, and then, just one. She wasn't even sure now, looking back, if they were her exact words or just a facsimile, close to the truth but subtly, significantly, different. In this way families brew their own legends.

It started south, in the West Country, with parents. The heat of the day ebbed into long shadows as the bottle ran low. Conversations that all day had danced around the crib now lunged into focus: *the clock's ticking, never a right time, you can't imagine the joy.*

Their usual rebuttals. *Seven billion and counting, every western child another 9,000 tonnes of carbon, mountains of fetid landfill from every pampered bottom, the things, the endless things of the Breeders.* Later, she cringes at their casual contempt - such rudeness to their hosts, their breeders – but reason is pitiless, unsentimental. *Everything's a military exercise for Breeders, they can never just go anywhere; the planning, the buying, the bringing of all the things, just to get lunch!* Brittle knowing laughter.

But you don't have to be like them. We had nothing, we managed. And we had to wash all the nappies. It's so much easier today.

And then there's the two of them. How much would be changed when two is three and the third is unknown? Who would risk something so precious? *Nobody ever says they regret it, how could they, but did you see he's sticking with that awful job, she's been on ADs for two years, they're moving out to the sticks, a two hour commute.*

The evening blooms, lights twinkle on glass, another bottle. *But if you miss this chance you could regret it for ever.* Then memories of babyhood, tiny hands, little fingers curling, a one bedroom flat, *We managed.* Feeding the ducks, on the swings for hours, splashing in puddles. *It was free, we were happy. It goes by so quickly.*

Aha, their adversaries have undone themselves. Because isn't that all it is, really? An endless tango with mortality. But the couple are still young enough, unfettered enough, poor enough, not to feel the beat. They feel no urge to leave a genetic imprint for the ages. This life is enough. Civilisations throughout millennia rise and fall until they're just grains of sand, blown in the wind and lost to the yawning black chasm of time. What matters one more zygote, blooming into life, pulsing and feeding in the soft wet darkness, a smudge on a scan, a heartbeat, a kick? Can they not see the futility?

The parents shake their heads sadly. *We can't explain it, until it happens to you, you can't understand.* The dance ends, a hollow win, all are defeated. The conversation rattles bright now towards goodbyes, a shiny slice of trips and work and telly.

Finally the couple glide north, the evening lowing into dusk, the road ahead slicing through fields of rapeseed like a knife through butter, the air thick with its heady scent. The old car rattles through the gears; this journey eats their credit.

I can't believe they did it again. It's like an obsession.

She sits silent and weighs the moment. Suddenly, but maybe always, the script she helped to write no longer reads true. *We can't explain it, until it happens to you.* And she knows this: that never to hold a baby, her baby, to hold a warm solid body in her arms, to lift her child to see the sea and kiss a milky head, would be a terrible loss, a physical pain. And that this loss, this loss of something she's never had - how can that be? *We can't explain it* – would be more than she could bear. A loss that would echo down the years. That the years would go by slower, emptier, harder as a result.

Every time we come here, it's the same routine. They just don't get what we're saying. Every time the same arguments. It just makes it harder to come down here.

Still she sits silent. After all that has been said this evening, and so many evenings before, how to rewrite the script? If she changes the words, the future tilts to a different horizon: what if they can't find their way back?

Her silence deepens with the dusk. Words have power; she feels this deeply. Like seeds, once strewn they take on a life of their own that cannot be taken back. What if she speaks her heart's desire and the words, like a curse in a fairy tale, sour the sweetness of their life. But, a deeper fear, what if words left unspoken still wield power? What punishment then?

The universe is pitiless, she reminds herself, it is not out to trick her, or punish her, for wanting more or for being a-feared. No, it is she that wields the power to harm herself, by yearning silently, grievously. These words need air.

She takes a deep breath and pulls her future close. In the gloaming he cannot see her shape shift; her transition, like a seed, is in darkness.

Actually, I'd quite like a baby...

And so a legend is born. Years later, the word echoes back, a talisman for good cheer in the face of the exhaustion, the noise, the mess, the bills, the fears, the too tight shoes, the scuffed knees, the fevers, and yes, the things. *Actually*.

And, every time, like a well-rehearsed catechism, an incantation to keep them safe, she says the same thing. I never spoke truer or wiser. *This is the best thing we have ever done.*

And she means it. She spoke her heart's desire and it came true. Words have that power. Actually.

Afterword

by

Athena Lamnisos

The Eve Appeal

'Can you say the word vagina without being embarrassed?'

This was one of the questions I was asked in my interview for CEO of The Eve Appeal. Not a standard interview question I know, but it made total sense when becoming the head of the UK's only gynaecological cancer research charity. I'm aware that many women, including some of my friends and family, might have hesitated when asked that question. I know just how vital it is to raise awareness and understanding of these cancers in order to remove all the stigma and embarrassment that surrounds them.

A dictionary definition of vagina is very straightforward: 'the part of a woman's body that connects her outer sex organs to her womb' - it's an anatomical term, and should be used without embarrassment or shame.

At The Eve Appeal we know that this is far from being the case. Women are not only embarrassed to talk about gynaecological symptoms, some age groups are completely lacking in information about gynaecological issues. Our work to increase awareness of the symptoms of all five gynaecological cancers (womb, ovarian, cervical, vulval and vaginal) and overcome the stigma that surrounds talking about them will save women's lives.

We are ambitious for a future where no woman delays seeing her GP due to the intimate nature of her symptoms. A future where women of all ages know about the early signs and symptoms of all five gynaecological cancers and know where to go for more information. At The Eve Appeal, we encourage all women to listen to their bodies, look out for any changes and see their doctor if something does not feel right. I'm outraged that women are literally dying from embarrassment.

One thing is very clear to me - gynaecological cancers don't discriminate; they can affect women at any age. Nearly 20,000 women in the UK are diagnosed with a gynaecological cancer and almost 8,000 die within five years.

The statistics are brutal and what's really tragic is that so little has changed for some of the gynae cancers where so much progress has been made for other health conditions. Deaths from lung cancer and heart diseases have halved since 1970. Over the same period of time, deaths from breast cancer have gone down by 40%. If you're diagnosed today with ovarian cancer, your mortality rate is pretty much the same as it would have been in 1970. Deaths from ovarian cancer have decreased by less than 2%.

So these are the statistics that The Eve Appeal is campaigning to change – through funding medical research and raising awareness.

So after you've closed this book, don't forget to open up on gynae cancers. You just might have a conversation that helps save a life.

Better still, open up your wallet!

Text GCAM15 with your amount e.g. GCAM15 10 to 70070 to donate £10 to The Eve Appeal.

www.eveappeal.org.uk/donate-now
Twitter: @theeveappeal
Facebook: TheEveAppeal
Instagram: EveAppeal

About the Contributors

The stories for *We need to talk* were selected from a open writing competition hosted by Kindred.

The judges were:

Susan Armstrong, Conville & Walsh
Anne C. Perry, Hodder & Stoughton
Athena Lamnisos, The Eve Appeal
Anastasia Scott, Kindred

Thank you to the hundreds of people who sent us their stories, as well as to the judges and other volunteers who made this book possible.

Adam Christopher Smith is a journalist and writer originally from Maidenhead, Berkshire, now living in Cardiff. He enjoys eating avocados, watching foreign dramas and hanging out with cats and dogs.

Amy McLellan is a freelance journalist whose assignments have taken her from busy Tehran to oil rigs in the North Sea to the remote Faroe Islands. She now lives in north Shropshire with her writer husband and three young children. Time permitting, Amy loves yoga, walking and writing.

Andreina Cordani is a freelance writer based in Dorset and spends her time contributing to women's magazines such as *Cosmopolitan* and *Prima*, working on her novel and having fascinating chats about trains with her two-year-old son. She also reviews books and blogs about her writing life on www.acordani.com

Bridie Wilkinson is a Studio Executive in the Art department of Hodder & Stoughton. Living in London, she is a big enthusiast of knitwear and stories, in their many, many forms.

Charlotte Brazier is a features writer at HotSpot Media and lives in Birmingham. She spent most of her childhood writing weird little stories in her bedroom and is astounded that she now does this for an actual job. Her hobbies include cello, piano and cats.

Daisy Buchanan is a journalist who lives in Greenwich with her fiancé, Dale. She writes about mental health, dating and reality telly. When she's not gazing into a laptop she likes making mac'n'cheese and making friends with the dogs she meets when she's running very slowly around her local park.

Eleanor Pender is the Communications Executive for the Edinburgh UNESCO City of Literature Trust. She lives in Edinburgh, and outside of work, Eleanor loves cinema, regularly visiting The Cameo, and is also a member of spoken word collective, Inky Fingers.

Johanna Jowers is a spokesperson for the Let Toys Be Toys campaign. She lives in Kent with her family, where she writes, sings in a worship band and dabbles in local community politics.

Katie McCrory is a design strategist, bridging communications and business innovation to help organisations understand how they can do well by doing good. She splits her time between London and Copenhagen, spending most of her free time on her bicycle discovering new places to eat and drink with her equally cycling-minded husband.

Kim Curran has been an advertising copywriter for nearly 20 years, specialising in youth marketing. She is also the author of novels for young adults, including the Shifter trilogy and *Glaze*. She was nominated for the Sydney J Bounds, Best Newcomer Award, 2012, and her short story, 'A Woman Out of Time', was selected for the Tiptree Award Honor List, 2014. Her greatest achievement was when Tom Baker said a script she wrote was funny. He was being paid.

Lee-Anne Smith is a copywriter and content creator at The Verb Shop. She lives in London with her family and loves storytelling in all its forms, visiting museums and walking in the rain.

Milly Johnson was born, raised and still lives in Barnsley, South Yorkshire. As well as being an author of 11 published novels, 2 short story books and a novella, she is also a copywriter for the greetings card industry, a joke-writer, a columnist, after dinner speaker, poet, BBC newspaper reviewer and a sometimes BBC radio presenter. She writes about love, life, friendships and that little bit of the magic that sometimes crops up in real life. She likes owls and meringues and hates marzipan. She is very short.

Niall Alexander is an extra-curricular English teacher who reads and writes about all things weird and wonderful for Tor.com. He lives with about a bazillion books, his better half and a certain sleekit wee beastie in the central belt of bonnie Scotland.

Paul Wiseall is a marketing manager for one of the UK's largest data companies. He lives in London and doesn't like fish but could probably manage a salmon en croute if he was forced.

Robert Sharp works for English PEN, the writers' association campaigning for freedom of expression and literature across frontiers. His novella *The Good Shabti* was shortlisted for the Shirley Jackson Awards. He lives in Bromley with his family.

Rosanne Rabinowitz is a freelance sub-editor and writer living in south London. Her involvement with social media at Boycott Workfare, a campaign to abolish benefit sanctions and forced unpaid labour, provided much of the inspiration for 'Keep Them Rollin''. Rosanne has also contributed short fiction to anthologies such as *Horror Uncut: Tales of Social Insecurity and Economic Unease*, *Jews vs Aliens* and *Tales from the Vatican Vaults*. Her novella *Helen's Story* (PS Publishing) was shortlisted for the 2013 Shirley Jackson Awards. Visit rosannerabinowitz. wordpress.com for more information.

Sam Holl is a Client Service Director at Kindred, looking after a portfolio of PR and social media accounts. He loves writing but has never written fiction before, so is pleasantly surprised to be featuring in this collection.

Tom Hunter is the kind of marketing person who passionately believes his job is to help people discover cool things and enjoy new experiences. This is why he tends to work in and around the arts, culture and tourism sectors. He's also the Director of the Arthur C. Clarke Award, the UK's premier prize for science fiction literature, and works as a freelance journalist and events organiser.

After a career in women's magazines in London, *Tiffany Sherlock* is now a freelance features writer, living in the Lake District with her partner and 17-month-old daughter. In her limited free time, she enjoys swimming, stone carving and writing her first novel.

Tim Major is Director of Online Resources at Scholastic. He lives in Oxford with his wife and son. In his free time he writes science fiction – his short stories have been published in *Interzone* and SF anthologies. He blogs about writing and reading at www.cosycatastrophes. wordpress.com

Kindred is an independent creative agency in central London offering expertise in advertising, PR, social and digital design.

Recognised as one of the Best Workplaces in the UK, Kindred takes a people-centred approach to communications; listening to and learning from the people our campaigns are aimed at. After all, true insight comes from understanding people.

Learn more at www.kindredagency.com